She pressed her lips together. Tom was the only man she'd ever been with and she'd never looked past him, but now something was unraveling, taking hold of her senses. What would it be like with Joel? How would it feel? She wanted to know, needed to know. She took a breath, resting her hands on his chest. "Kiss me…"

His eyes darted to her mouth, a landscape of light and shade in his eyes. She slid her hands upward, to the sides of his neck and on until she was holding his face. "I want you to."

An animal noise rumbled in his throat and then his mouth was on hers. She closed her eyes, losing herself in the sweet caress of his lips.

"Emilie!" It was a ragged exclamation, and then his eyes were on hers. She felt the warm pad of his thumb moving over her cheekbone, a fresh tug of desire drawing tight in her belly. "Have you got any idea what you're doing to me…?"

She nodded. Her lips felt used, swollen, still hungry. "I do, because you're doing it to me, too…"

Dear Reader,

I can't believe that this is my fourth book for Harlequin Romance! I'm having so much fun inventing heartwarming, feel-good reads that I frequently have to pinch myself to check that I'm not dreaming!

This time we're off to the British Virgin Islands, to a tiny private island that I happened to see for sale when I was pondering locations for this story. As soon as I saw it, I knew that Buck Island would be the perfect setting for a romance of the "two people thrown together" type.

This is the first romance I've written about a place with which I'm not familiar, so I spent a lot of time researching online: the different beaches, the flora and fauna, places of interest, and so on. It's amazing how little of what I researched actually made it onto the page but it all feeds into the process, giving me a sense of place as I'm writing. I could draw a detailed map of my reimagined Buck Island and the neighbouring island of Tortola, that's for sure!

I hope you love this story as much as I loved writing it.

Ella x

Tycoon's Unexpected Caribbean Fling

Ella Hayes

Recycling programs
for this product may
not exist in your area.

ISBN-13: 978-1-335-56697-3

Tycoon's Unexpected Caribbean Fling

Copyright © 2021 by Ella Hayes

This edition published by arrangement with Harlequin Books S.A.

For questions and comments about the quality of this book,
please contact us at CustomerService@Harlequin.com.

Harlequin Enterprises ULC
22 Adelaide St. West, 40th Floor
Toronto, Ontario M5H 4E3, Canada
www.Harlequin.com

Printed in U.S.A.

After ten years as a television camerawoman, **Ella Hayes** started her own photography business so that she could work around the demands of her young family. As an award-winning wedding photographer, she's documented hundreds of love stories in beautiful locations, both at home and abroad. She lives in central Scotland with her husband and two grown-up sons. She loves reading, traveling with her camera, running and great coffee.

Books by Ella Hayes

Harlequin Romance

Her Brooding Scottish Heir
Italian Summer with the Single Dad
Unlocking the Tycoon's Heart

Visit the Author Profile page
at Harlequin.com for more titles.

For Phil

**Praise for
Ella Hayes**

"Ella Hayes has surpassed herself with this delightfully warm romance. It keeps a reader on their toes with its twists and turns. The characters are believable and you can actually visualize the scenes through the exquisite descriptions. This book ambushes your senses and takes the reader on a beautiful journey with heart-stopping moments. A wonderful relaxing read."

—*Goodreads* on *Italian Summer with the Single Dad*

CHAPTER ONE

EMILIE CLAYTON WRIGGLED her sandy toes and inspected her legs. They were turning a lovely shade of golden brown. She hitched her sarong a little higher and inspected the skin above her knees. That part was tanning nicely too, but exactly how it was happening was a mystery.

Maybe she'd been catching the sun during her daily walks from the cottage to the house. Not on the path that wove through the gumbo limbo trees, where the sunlight splashed chaotically on to the giant, hand-shaped leaves of the under storey, but rather, on the long upward climb to the rear entrance of the luxury residence where there was no shade at all.

The sun always felt warm on her bare calves as she made her way up the pale granite steps, so that would probably explain it, although, the motor launch was another possibility. She always wore shorts when she was going over to

Tortola for provisions and she never sat under the canopy.

She rearranged the sarong over her legs and looked up, gazing at the jewel-bright sea and the distant, hazy green hills of the neighbouring Caribbean islands. It didn't matter anyway. However it was happening, the deepening colour on her legs was completely accidental because there'd been no time for sunbathing since she'd arrived on Buck Island.

For the past three weeks she'd been flat out in the kitchen, creating exotic dishes to satisfy the exacting clientele. Breakfasts had to consist of a freshly prepared buffet with hot and cold options, lunches had to be light and exquisite, and dinners had to match anything that her former boss, celebrated chef Michel Lefevre, could have produced in his famous London restaurant Le Perroquet. Initially, she'd been nervous, not because she lacked the culinary skills, but because she'd been doing everything herself and she wasn't used to that. She was used to Tom being there, working around her, anticipating her every move. He'd always had her back in the kitchen, and out of it, until… Her insides twisted sharply. *Tom!* Four months had passed since he'd ripped her world apart, but it still hurt because it wasn't just Tom, it was everything that went with him…

She hugged her knees in tight, pushing the thoughts away, listening to the rustling palms and the lapping waves and the comical kazoo-like call of a passing seabird. The thing was, in spite of her nerves, she *had* prevailed—more than prevailed if the compliments in the visitors' book were anything to go by, so that was something!

She pushed herself up, brushing off her sarong and tightening it around her waist. Of course, having Melinda there had made a world of difference. With her wide, white smile and her easy, maternal manner, Melinda's lilting voice and wicked sense of humour had helped to keep her calm, even on the night when the twelve guests, between them, had ordered six different mains.

She walked towards the water's edge, feeling a smile unfolding inside. Melinda and her husband, Erris, were so much more than housekeeper and site manager. They were her neighbours—their cottage was five minutes' walk from her own—but in just three weeks they'd also become dear friends, showing her the ropes, looking after her. They were warm, family-orientated people. Their son, Anton, ran his own SUV hire place in Road Town and was also the most sought-after car mechanic on Tortola. In his spare time, he was a Moko

Jumbie stilt-dancing trainer, teaching young-sters as well as performing himself with his troupe. Melinda had shown her videos. Crazy dance moves, fantastic costumes. Her mind had been blown! Anton's sister, Kesney, ran her own soap-making business using locally harvested sea salt. Kesney and her husband, Will, were expecting their first baby and Melinda and Erris were bursting with excitement. Buck Island was only a short hop from Tortola, but it was clear that they missed being around their loved ones.

Maybe that was why Melinda mothered *her* at every opportunity, why she'd frogmarched her out of the kitchen that morning telling her to take some time off before she collapsed with exhaustion. At least, that was what her eyes had been saying. What had come out of her mouth was, 'Get out from under my feet— I've got to get things ready for Mr Larsson.'

Time off! For a moment she zoned out, en-joying the warm slosh of the water around her feet, then she looked along the beach. At the far end, a cluster of boulders lazed in the shallows as if they'd tumbled drunkenly down the hill on which the sleek, modern residence stood. Until today she'd only had time to ex-plore the forty-acre island in snatches, but now she was free for a couple of hours. That was plenty of time to walk right round the island without hurrying!

She started walking, absently pulling her swim-dampened hair forwards and twisting it into a rope. Larsson sounded like a Swedish name, she thought. Scandinavian anyway. According to Melinda, he'd taken the whole place for three weeks and he hadn't invited any guests. *Weird!* But Melinda said that it happened sometimes, that it was pointless trying to fathom the whims of the rich and privileged. Still, a six-bedroomed luxury residence on a private island seemed excessive for one person, and as for her own role as chef...

She stopped to watch a big brown pelican skimming over the water with lazy flaps of its wings. Beyond it, in the distance, a catamaran was speeding along, one hull rising into the air. She walked on, pushing loose strands of salt-sticky hair away from her face. Catering for one person was going to leave her seriously underemployed! Perfect if she'd *wanted* to have time on her hands, but the whole point of taking this crazy contract had been to keep herself busy, too busy to think about what was happening on the other side of the world, with Tom.

And Rachel...

She clamped her lips together, walking

faster. *Tom and Rachel!* Imagining them together... Choosing paint colours, buying stuff, making plans. *Nesting!* She felt a sob rising in her throat, felt her feet turning to clay. She looked down, swallowing hard. *Breathe!* Barely an hour into her afternoon off and Tom was in her head with her best friend, Rachel. *So-called!* This was what happened when she had nothing to do! Three busy weeks had left her no time for thinking, not even at night because she'd been out like a light as soon as her head had hit the pillow, but now it was open season. With time on her hands she was going to be a sitting duck and that wasn't what she'd signed up for! Admittedly, the job description had stated that she'd be catering for *up to* twelve guests at any one time, but in her wildest imaginings she hadn't thought she'd be catering for one guest for three whole weeks! Why, oh, why wasn't lonely Larsson bringing eleven hungry friends? Would it have been too much to ask? Now, because of him, she was going to be twiddling her thumbs, stewing in her own juices and that was absolutely the last thing...

A sudden metallic clank stopped her midstride. She looked up, felt her breath catching. A sports catamaran was nosing its way on to the beach a few metres away. There was a hearty splash and then a tall, fair-haired man wearing orange swim shorts and a life vest appeared from behind the sail and began hauling the vessel up on to the sand.

She licked her lips, tasting salt. An odd bristling sensation was taking her over, pulsing through her veins. Buck Island was a private island with private beaches. It wasn't a free-for-all! It wasn't there for the random parking of boats—or catamarans for that matter—by any Tom, Dick or Harry who happened to be passing. Larsson wouldn't be happy, that was for sure. He'd booked a private island presumably because he wanted to be private. There was only one thing for it: she would have to give this fellow his marching orders!

She checked her sarong, then advanced towards the gleaming catamaran and the man who was now tugging at a rope which was attached to something at the top of the mast. She took a deep breath. 'Excuse me, but this is a *private* beach!'

No reaction.

She sucked in another lungful of air. Perhaps he hadn't heard her. The sail was flapping, probably drowning her out. She moved nearer, taking in the swell of his biceps, the tattoo line running down the length of his inner arm and the smattering of stubble around his jaw, which was fair, just like his thick, deliciously tousled hair. She ran her tongue over her lower lip. It was tempting just to stand and watch him... *Stop!* Seconds ago she'd been choking back tears over Tom and now she was ogling the beach trespasser! What was wrong with her? She swallowed hard. The stranger *was,* irrefutably, the most gorgeous man she'd ever laid eyes on, but that was incidental. He was still trespassing. She steadied her feet, cleared her throat and tried again. 'Excuse me...?'

This time his shoulders jerked and then the rope slipped cleanly through his hands. For a beat he seemed to freeze, then he caught it again and turned round. Cool blue-grey eyes fastened on hers. 'Hello, yes?'

She sank her teeth into her lower lip. Maybe opening with a simple hello or a jaunty *Ahoy, sailor!* would have been better, but it was too late now. The rather confrontational *Excuse me?* was out there and clearly the fair-haired stranger was needled. Although, to his credit, he looked as if he was trying to hide it. Something about his mouth, a tiny upward movement in one corner, didn't quite match his steely gaze.

She moistened her lips. Michel Lefevre had been the master of steely gazes, so she wasn't fazed although, unaccountably, her fingers seemed to have drifted to the halter strap of her swimsuit. She dropped her hand, shifting her stance, praying that the warmth she could feel in her cheeks wasn't visible from where he was standing. 'I'm sorry for shouting, but you didn't hear me the first time…'

The tension in his face seemed to melt a little, the lines around his eyes smoothing themselves out, and suddenly all the words she'd been going to say were dissolving on her tongue. He might have looked arrogant as he'd dragged the catamaran on to the beach, but there was something discernibly lost about him, something behind his eyes that seemed to call for a softer approach.

She gave a little shrug. 'I didn't mean to startle you.'

'It's fine.' He glanced at the mast. 'The sail's noisy…it can be hard to hear…' His fingers toyed with the rope and then he was looking at her again, a glimmer of confusion behind his eyes. 'So… Who are you?'

The tables seemed to have been turned. Somehow, *she* was the one having to explain herself and, under his steady gaze, she couldn't even think of how to reclaim the advantage. She pressed her lips together, hooking a wind-blown lock of hair behind her ear. 'I'm Emilie.'

'Right.' Even more confusion in his eyes. 'And you're here to…?'

This definitely wasn't playing out the way she'd intended. Suddenly her mouth was dry and there was an odd fluttering sensation in her belly. Somehow the stranger with the foreign accent and the body of a Viking god was dismantling her bravado piece by piece…

Viking?

Intent blue-grey eyes… Thick fair hair, longer on top… Inky line running all the way down his muscular arm to the wristband of his expensive, branded watch… Swedish accent! *Oh, God!* How could she have been so stupid? The man she'd nearly ordered off the beach was lonely Larsson.

Joel Larsson suddenly realised that he was holding his breath, the way he did when he was testing a program. That moment…pressing the final key…wondering if the firewall would crumble or kick in as it should… But computers were an easy hack compared to deciphering the myriad expressions playing across Emilie's face. It had been a simple enough question he'd asked, yet she seemed to be struggling. He licked his lips. 'Emilie…?'

She blinked, then her expression was softening, rearranging itself around the warmest, loveliest smile he'd ever seen. 'I'm here to welcome you to Buck Island!'

He felt his mouth falling open and closed it again quickly. 'But—'

'You *are* Mr. Larsson?' Smiling had warmed her eyes—hazel eyes—making them sparkle.

He nodded, not trusting himself to speak. He hadn't been expecting a welcome party; he hadn't been expecting anyone, except for the cheery guy who had met him at the airport and taken him to the boat hire place. Erris—that was what he'd said his name was—said he did the fetching and carrying, maintenance and suchlike. Erris had taken charge of his luggage, assuring him that he'd find it in his room when he arrived. A maintenance guy was one thing, but now there was an 'Emilie' greeting him on the beach, wearing a fetching swimsuit and a sarong. Surely Nils wouldn't have— *No!* Even in full-throttle best man mode Nils wouldn't have pulled a stunt like that. Still, the fact remained: there was a beautiful girl standing in front of him, waiting for him to say something. He took a breath, stepped forward and held out his hand. 'Please! Call me Joel.'

'Pleased to meet you, Joel.' She shook his hand quickly, then stepped back, a minute flare of uncertainty in her eyes.

He checked himself. Was his shock manifesting as unfriendliness? Did she think he'd been ignoring her before…? He hadn't. It was just that the sail had been obscuring his view of the beach as he'd come in and, since he hadn't been expecting to see anyone, he hadn't looked about. He'd just got on with the business of pulling the boat up on to the sand, lost in his own head and in the mechanics of what he was doing. And now her eyes were cloudy and maybe it was his fault.

Damn! If only he'd paid more attention to what Nils had said, then he might have had an inkling of who Emilie was and what was going on, but he hadn't exactly been in the best headspace of late. It was entirely possible that minor details could have sailed right over his head. He searched his memory, could almost feel Nils's hand on his back.

'You'll love Buck Island, Joel. It's paradise! You'll be able to sail every day, chill out…get your head straight again… And you'll have the whole place to yourself. I've made sure of that! It's the best cancelled wedding present I could think of.'

Relief washed over him. At least he hadn't lost his mind completely. There were no crossed wires; Nils had definitely said that he'd have the whole place to himself. So in that case, where did Emilie fit in? And how could she possibly have known that he'd be landing on *this* beach at exactly *this* moment when he'd only decided five minutes ago that he was probably too jetlagged to sail for the whole afternoon and ought to come in before he did something stupid, like capsize. He held in a sigh. It seemed that he was drowning regardless, not that he intended to let it show. She might have blindsided him, but he still had his pride.

He unzipped his life vest and shrugged it off, shooting her a covert glance. Her swimsuit was low cut, the full swell of her breasts hard to ignore. *She* was hard to ignore—period—because for some reason she wasn't leaving and that meant that he was going to have to make conversation, at least until he could figure out what the hell was going on. He stepped towards the boat, glancing at the mast. 'Do you sail, Emilie?'

'No.' She gave a little shrug. 'I've never...'

For some reason, her words trailed away. At the lower edge of his vision, he could see her toe sketching a line in the sand. He raked his teeth over his lower lip, trying to stop his eyes mapping out the ample curve of her hips and her breasts. 'So—' he shifted on his feet, clearing his throat so that his voice would actually work '—what do you do?'

'I…erm…' She folded her arms across her chest, eyes holding his for a long second, and then suddenly a tiny spark ignited in their depths. 'Oh! You mean *here*…what do I do here? On the island?'

He nodded.

She smiled hesitantly. 'I'm the chef.'

Chef?

'Breakfast… Lunch… Dinner…' Her smile seemed to be fading. 'Afternoon tea…?' Her eyes were widening. 'Anything you want…'

'Cool—' he rubbed the back of his neck '—I mean, thanks.' He forced out a smile, then turned to the boat, mechanically liberating the mainsail. His chest felt tight. His pulse was bounding. *Kristus! This* was exactly why he needed *not* to be with people! He was morose and churlish, and…lost. He hadn't been anticipating a chef and he hadn't been quick enough to hide it, and now he'd made Emilie feel uncomfortable which was the last thing he'd meant to do. It wasn't her fault. *He* was the one who hadn't read the brochure Nils had given him. He'd just assumed… *Skit!*

He hefted the sail on to the sand, laying it out ready for folding. Nils had done a nice thing, a very generous thing, but it was suddenly looking as if his private island escape wasn't going to be that private after all. A sharp ache dug him in the ribs. After everything he'd been through with Astrid, he wanted to be alone, *needed* to be alone to process his thoughts. He was perfectly able to make his own breakfast, lunch and dinner. He didn't want, or need, a personal chef!

A sudden gust tore the sail from his hands, carrying it scuttling, crablike, up the beach. He sprinted after it, slipping and scuffling in the soft sand until he was right there, sinking to his knees, laying a hand on it, then somehow Emilie was there beside him, on her knees too, grabbing at the flapping clew, her long, dark hair lifting, billowing around her face, revealing her smooth neck, a tiny gold cuff on the rim of her left ear. For half a beat her eyes held his and in that instant the wind gusted again, carrying the sail off beyond his reach. He rocked back on his heels. *'Skit!'*

'If that was my fault, I'm sorry.' She was panting slightly, taming her hair with her hands, twisting it into a rope. 'I was trying to help!'

If she was sorry, then why was there a smile hovering at the corners of her lovely mouth? He shrugged. 'It wasn't your fault. I wasn't holding it properly.'

Her eyes widened. 'We can try again…?'

It was hard not to get lost in the sweet planes

of her face, in the smooth arc of her dark eyebrows. Those eyes… He pushed a hand through his hair. She was the chef he didn't need, a *distraction* he didn't need, but when it came to runaway sails, two people were better than one. He rubbed the sand off his hands. 'We'll have to, because if it gets into the trees, it could get ripped.' He glanced at the sail, barely ten metres away, undulating softly in the breeze. 'Just grab whatever you can okay, and—' it was hard not to stare at her mouth '—thanks.'

Amusement twinkled in her eyes. 'Don't thank me yet. It could all go Pete Tong.'

'Pete Tong?'

'It means wrong.' She grinned. 'It's like rhyming slang.'

'Pete Tong! I get it.' He held in a smile. 'Right… Let's go!' He launched himself at the sail, catching the tack, making sure that he had it in both hands before looking up. Emilie was fighting with the other corner, bending over it, giving him a bird's eye view of her smooth, full breasts and the dusky hollow of her cleavage. He swallowed hard. Looking was wrong, but it was impossible to tear his eyes away, impossible to stop them wandering over her hips and her narrow waist. She was curvy, like an hourglass, not at all like Astrid—

'I've got the pointy bit under control!'

Flushed cheeks, lustrous eyes. She looked so ridiculously triumphant that, for a moment, he forgot everything. He felt a smile coming and it wasn't a tight smile, or a forced smile, but the real deal. 'Great! Keep tight hold, okay, and… for future reference, it's not called the pointy bit. It's called the clew.' He pressed his lips together, watching her face, counting down in his head…

She inspected the piece of sail in her hands and then she looked up, her cheeks lifting into a smile. 'You mean I've actually got a clue? That'd be a first!'

He laughed. 'Never grows old.'

So *that* was lonely Larsson! Emilie walked back the way she'd come, pleased to be putting some distance between herself and the delectable man who'd sailed on to the beach right under her nose. She clenched her teeth, resisting the urge to grind them. What had got into her? She'd marched right up to Buck Island's newest guest, full of self-righteous indignation, intending to send him on his way. As if she'd even had the right to do such a thing! Thank God she'd realised who he was in the nick of time. And if Joel Larsson hadn't quite bought into her whole welcome routine, then at least he'd had the good grace not to say anything.

She chewed her lip. Why couldn't he have arrived on the motor launch with Erris, with luggage, and wearing actual clothes like all the other guests had done? Instead, he'd sailed in on a breeze, out of the blue, and from the moment he'd turned around and fixed his eyes on hers, the sand beneath her feet might just as well have been quicksand. And when he'd taken off his life vest, revealing his broad, smooth chest and those delectable V-shaped muscles arrowing into his bright orange board shorts, God help her, it had been impossible to concentrate on a single word he was saying.

She stopped, suddenly compelled to look back. There was no tall, muscular figure on the beach now, but the catamaran seemed to be further away from the water than it had been when she'd left. He must have dragged it towards the palm trees before heading up to the house, the house that ought to have been filled with twelve people, not one.

She closed her eyes, picturing his... Blue-grey, more blue than grey when the sun struck his irises at just the right angle, and a warm, glinting blue when he'd smiled. Why was he alone, a man like that? It didn't make sense.

And why had he seemed so surprised when she'd told him she was the chef? Admittedly, a swimsuit and sarong didn't exactly scream *Cook*, but even so, his reaction had suggested that he wasn't expecting a chef at all. *Bizarre!* Who would book an exclusive island escape and *not* know what they were paying for?

She dropped down on to the sand, sliding her toes into its warm, deep softness. *Joel Larsson!* Cool as a glacier, but with the sail in his hands she'd seen mischief flaring in his eyes. A lighter side. The way his eyebrows had quirked.

'Never grows old.'

His chuckle had been deep and throaty. Genuine. It had been a nice surprise…his laughter…hers… The way they'd laughed together, melting all the ice.

'It's C-L-E-W,' he'd explained afterwards, 'not C-L-U-E.'

And then he'd talked her through the whole anatomy of the mainsail as they'd folded it up—head and foot and tack and clew—but she hadn't minded. Talking had discharged a little of the static she'd felt crackling between them every time their eyes had locked for longer than a moment or two. *Static!* She hadn't felt anything like that for a long time. It was unsettling.

She scooped up a handful of sand, letting it fall streaming through her fist. Being attracted to Joel wasn't a crime—he *was* gorgeous—but he was also a guest on the island. Even if she'd been the type to consider a little holiday romance, which she wasn't, dallying with a guest was completely out of the question. It wasn't a stipulation of her contract; it was simple professionalism—and the last time she'd checked she *still* was a professional, even if she no longer had a restaurant, or a partner, or a best friend…

She swallowed hard. That was what she'd been turning over in her head before Joel appeared. All the things she'd lost: all those years with Tom, all that *time*… And she'd been worrying that if she wasn't run off her feet, if she wasn't too busy to think, then those memories and thoughts would torment her. As the catamaran had touched the beach, she'd been simmering with all that hurt and anger and it had bubbled up inside her, sent her marching up to Joel, because in that moment, letting those feelings breach the surface, *doing* something with them, even if it was only ordering a trespasser off the beach, had seemed better than pushing them back down. But Joel was innocent. *He* wasn't the problem.

She closed her eyes, listening to the waves

spilling on to the shore. If only she could view the prospect of having time to herself more positively. After all, this was paradise island! Green and golden, and turquoise. Warm and peaceful, and... *Lonely.* Her stomach clenched, then churned slowly. Before she'd even met him, she'd christened Joel *'Lonely Larsson'*, but maybe that said more about *her* than it did about him. He might well have come to the island by himself because he *liked* solitude, whereas *she* never had. For her, solitude meant loneliness. It meant being the odd one out. It meant being unwanted...

She trailed her fingers through the sand. It was how she'd felt at home, growing up. Her older twin sisters had always been locked together in a way that had excluded her. The seven-year gap that separated her from them hadn't helped... She bit her lips together. It was obvious that she hadn't been planned. Her friends had all had siblings who were closer in age, siblings they could hang out with even if they didn't always get along. She'd asked her parents about it once and they'd said that *of course* she'd been planned, then they'd laughed, said that she was the evidence of a healthy relationship. *That* had definitely been too much information, even if, on reflection, it was true.

Her parents were one of those couples who'd always seemed to live in one another's pockets. They'd been on parent–teacher committees together—chair and vice-chair. They'd been members of the same hiking club. They liked the same food, the same bands, the same movies, and, now that they lived in Abu Dhabi, they were golf partners and bridge partners.

Pairs! Partners! That was what she'd known, growing up. It could have moulded her differently, made her fiercely independent, but it hadn't. Instead, it had given her a map to follow. And she'd followed that map religiously, hadn't she? Attaching herself to anyone who gave her the time of day. Always needing a best friend. Safety in numbers, better together—those were the pillars she'd clung to. It was why what had happened between Tom and Rachel felt like the ultimate betrayal.

She stabbed her fingers hard into the sand, recoiling as a something sharp pricked her fingertip. She felt around it, excavating. It had to be a conch! These islands were famous for them. She'd read that conches were signifiers of optimism, courage and hope, all things she desperately needed! She freed it, brushing the sand off. It was lovely. Pale and ridged on the outside with little spurs sticking out, curving upwards. She turned it over, dipping her fingertip into the smooth, pink space that was once the creature's doorway. A doorway to optimism, courage and hope…? She closed her fist around it, felt the spikes impaling her palm.

'We need to talk…'

She swallowed hard. At least she wasn't crying. Tom's voice, in her head, saying those words, usually tore her heart in two, but now, for some reason, she was thinking about the shell and the solitary creature that had lived inside it. She opened her hand. The little soft-bodied creature had built itself quite a fortress. She chewed her lip. Maybe she should do the same. She'd started going out with Tom when she was seventeen. She'd never stood on her own two feet, steering her own course. Perhaps Joel Larsson's solitude was a blessing! With a dramatically reduced workload for the next three weeks, she could use the time to reset…to try find out who she was, who she *could* be… She'd have time to grow her own shell and learn how to be alone. Not lonely, but alone and happy!

She scrambled to her feet, clasping the little shell tightly. For a dizzying moment, Joel's steady blue-grey gaze filled her head, but she pushed it away. She liked Joel, but she couldn't allow herself to think of him in a romantic way. She was done with men, done with love. It was time to put herself in the centre.

CHAPTER TWO

JOEL SLID HIS empty suitcase into the closet and closed the door, turning to look at the vast, airy bedroom that was going to be his for the next three weeks.

It was larger than their—correction—*his* bedroom in Stockholm, which was painted in shades of grey and cream. This room was white, with dark glowing furniture and a mellow wooden floor. The upholstery and curtains were a lively, tropical green, but it wasn't overdone; there was just enough colour to brighten the canvas. It was all very pleasant, with its mingling scents of clean bedlinen and warm wax polish.

He breathed in slowly, felt his shoulders loosening, a vague sensation of unfurling. Jetlag kicking in, he decided, fatigue claiming him at last. Maybe he'd overdone it a bit, hiring the catamaran straight from the airport and sailing himself to the island. But the two flights he'd taken to get here had felt interminable and he'd been desperate to breathe fresh air, to feel sunshine on his face and a breeze on his skin. And of course then, on the beach, there'd been the unexpected additional exertion of capturing the runaway sail: going after it, catching it, losing it again because of…

He crossed to sit on the ottoman that hugged the foot of the wide bed. *Emilie!* She was the reason he'd fumbled the sail. When she'd caught his eye for that tiniest of moments, he'd felt something shuttling between them, something that had skewed his senses and turned his bones to rubber. And then the sail had flown up the beach again, and they'd caught it together…and she'd been laughing about the clew. After that he'd had to keep on talking, telling her about the sail as she'd helped him to fold it, because otherwise he'd have lost himself completely in her sparkling hazel eyes and her luscious mouth, those sweetly curving lips…

He blew out a long breath. He hadn't been expecting Emilie, the chef, or Melinda, the housekeeper, for that matter. Melinda had given him a tour of the place shortly after he'd arrived. Full of smiles, she'd shown him the sitting room with its shuttered picture windows that could be slid back, giving access to the sweeping deck outside, the cinema with its sumptuous leather recliners, the library, the games room, the gym, the dining room, then she'd taken him outside so he could see the infinity pool and the terrace, and the panoramic views. Finally, she'd led him up the stairs and into the master suite, offering to unpack his suitcase if he wanted—*as if*—and then she'd said that when he was through with unpacking and freshening up, there'd be drinks and appetisers waiting for him on the terrace.

He bent to pick up the battered loafers he'd kicked off earlier. When Nils had told him that he'd booked a house on a private island he'd pictured something smaller, less luxurious, not a place like this, with rooms for everything and a speedboat for his personal use. He shook his head. He might have guessed! Nils lived extravagantly and was generous to a fault. It wouldn't have crossed his mind to find a more modest set up. He sighed. Melinda had definitely picked up on his incredulity. She'd barely been able to hide her amusement as she'd been showing him around. If only he'd read that damn brochure, he'd have known what to expect. He wouldn't have looked like such an idiot!

Dumskalle!

He toyed with his loafers, fingering the

faded leather. But he *was* an idiot, wasn't he? Stupid enough to have thought that his life as a husband had been about to start.

Astrid... Pale-lipped in the doorway. *'Joel, we need to talk...'*

He felt his pulse fading, then thudding on thickly, filling his ears, filling his throat. Eight weeks! Astrid had called off their wedding just eight weeks before the big day, throwing away eleven whole years together—*no*—more than that, because he'd been with Astrid from when they were teenagers. And her reason? He felt the sudden drag of dizziness. *Johan!* His own brother!

He gritted his teeth, swallowing hard. Way to capsize the boat! Way to dislocate the bones of a life! No wonder there was a humming black space where his heart used to be. Maybe his body was protecting him somehow, releasing an anaesthetic hormone into his bloodstream to stop the pain. But it was going on too long and he was sick of waiting for the pain to shred him. He *wanted* to feel it because he deserved to. He hadn't paid enough attention to Astrid, or to their life together. He'd been lazy, taken everything for granted. It was as if the diamond ring he'd slid on to Astrid's finger all those years ago had absolved him from thinking about love.

Instead, he'd dedicated himself to building his business and then when *he'd* felt it was time, he'd nudged Astrid into setting a date for their wedding. And she had. She'd booked a wedding planner, bought a dress, booked their honeymoon. It had all been going so well and then… Tightness clawed at his chest. He'd always been the quiet one, the middle child of five, the lone wolf. He'd always felt separate, and he'd been happy to *be* separate, but now it wasn't *his* choice. He was stranded. On the margins. Even if he'd wanted to talk to his family, he couldn't, because Johan *was* his family and he couldn't find the words anyway, couldn't make sense of his feelings and the numbness. He was lost…unable to focus on anything.

He took a deep breath and dropped his shoes on to the floor, working his feet into them slowly. He'd focused on Emilie, though, hadn't he? Shamelessly, he allowed his gaze to travel over her body while she'd been busy with the sail. Hard not to. He was only human and Emilie *was* utterly desirable, but what did it say about him, or about his feelings for Astrid? Feeling such a raw attraction for someone just weeks after losing the love of his life couldn't be right. There was obviously something deeply wrong with him.

He sighed, staring at a patch of sunlight on the floor until it was a blur. *Emilie!* Her eyes, her smile, the way her sarong had hugged her hips… He felt his insides tightening, heat rising. Surely this craving had to be a rebound kind of thing, just the numb, dead part of himself needing to feel something primal, like simple, unadulterated lust. He forced himself to his feet. That had to be it! On the beach, she'd taken him by surprise, like that Bond girl in *Doctor No*. She was a fantasy, that was all, and the spark he'd felt shuttling between them, the fire it had ignited inside him, would just have to burn itself out, because he wasn't a holiday fling kind of guy, and he wasn't in the right frame of mind for anything more than that.

Emilie was an indulgence he couldn't afford. He'd come to the island to take stock of his life, to get his head straight again and, since just looking at her bent his head—and everything else—out of shape, giving her a wide berth was his only option.

He moved to the door. Maybe keeping out of her way wouldn't be so hard. She was the chef, so as long as he kept himself away from the kitchen, he'd be fine. He raked his hands through his hair, then reached for the door handle. Melinda had said something about drinks on the terrace and, after the day's shocks and surprises, a drink suddenly seemed like a great idea.

'What are you making?' Melinda was eyeing the mound of floury dough on the work surface suspiciously, her eyebrows arching all the way into the furrows on her forehead.

Emilie smiled. 'Dinner rolls.'

'You haven't made those before.' For some reason, Melinda's lips were pursing.

'No, I haven't, not here anyway...' She kneaded the dough steadily, turning it round by degrees, stretching it, enjoying the elastic feel of it in her fingers. It was her grandmother who'd first introduced her to baking when she was about ten. They'd spent many a rainy afternoon making gingerbread men and cupcakes, then later, at home, after her sisters had left to go to university, she'd tried her hand at other things, discovered that she really did have a knack. Back then, she'd made bread all the time, especially on Sunday mornings. She looked up, catching Melinda's eye. 'I just had a notion...'

'Hmm.'

The small utterance carried a weight that belied its size. It was hard not to smile. 'Don't you approve of dinner rolls?'

'Of course!' Melinda's eyes widened, then narrowed a little. 'I was just looking at the time, that's all...'

'There's time.' She glanced at the wall clock. 'These are quick to make. Fifteen minutes proving, twelve minutes baking, five minutes cooling. They can go to the table warm... they're nicer that way.'

'Uh-huh.'

That was a loaded tone if ever there was one! She looked up, shrugging. 'What...?'

Melinda smiled slowly, her voice lilting with implication. 'I always think of bread as a lovely, nurturing kind of comfort food...'

'Maybe it is—for some people!' She picked up her knife, started dividing the dough into pieces. She had no idea what Melinda was driving at, but she didn't mind talking about comfort food. Recent events had turned her into something of an expert. 'My favourite comfort food is chocolate cake—' she looked up '—with a thick chocolate ganache.'

'Mmm. Sounds heavenly.' Melinda took a single, pristine napkin out of a drawer, bumping it shut with her hip. 'Talking of heavenly, Mr Larsson is very handsome and very sexy, don't you think?'

Oh, God! Was Melinda matchmaking? She felt heat creeping up her throat towards her cheeks. She took a careful breath. 'I can't say I've noticed.'

Melinda laughed roundly. 'Then why are you blushing?'

'I'm not!' She looked down, carried on carving up the dough. 'I'm just hot from kneading the dough, that's all.' Her pulse was fluttering. If only she hadn't poured out her heartbreak over Tom to Melinda and Erris in that first week, she'd have been able to pretend that she had a boyfriend in England and was therefore uninterested in handsome, sexy guests. If she hadn't told Melinda that she'd 'bumped' into Joel on the beach, she would have been able to pretend that she didn't know what he looked like, but it was too late now. Melinda knew everything and, from the look on her face, she was only getting started.

'Are you trying to nurture handsome Mr Larsson with your soft…warm…' Melinda was purring out the adjectives '…delicious… dinner rolls?'

'What?' Her cheeks were prickling. 'No! Of course not! That's ridiculous!' What was more ridiculous was that her heart was thumping hard. What was wrong with her? It wasn't as if Melinda was right! Joel hadn't been in her mind at all when she'd added sugar and water to the yeast, or when she'd taken the flour canister from the larder, but somehow Melinda had struck a nerve and struck it hard.

She looked down, staring at the dough, breathing in the sweet-sour smell of yeast until she could taste it in the back of her throat, and it was rowing her back to her parents' kitchen on a long-ago Sunday morning... It was taking her freshly baked bread rolls from the oven. It was hot quick fingers lifting them off the tray. It was breathing in that heavenly aroma, heart racing with anticipation, waiting for her parents to appear. It was that moment when they'd turned to look at her with warm, delighted smiles...

Melinda's voice jerked her back. 'I was only playing with you.'

She blinked, then met Melinda's gaze. 'I know.' Melinda *was* mischievous, but she was also wise and warm, and wonderful. She felt a smile edging on to her lips. 'But we should probably talk about this...' She put the knife aside and scooped up a piece of dough, rolling in her hands. 'Does Erris know that you've got the feels for our guest?'

'Feels?' Melinda's mouth fell open and then she was laughing. 'Don't you be telling him any such thing—' she waggled her eyebrows '—he's a very jealous man.'

'Who's a very jealous man?' Erris's voice

ballooned into the kitchen by way of the scullery, then the man himself appeared, his blue checked shirt buttoned tightly over his ample girth, his smile every bit as wide and as white as Melinda's.

'It's a private conversation—' Melinda tipped her a wink, then turned to her husband '—nothing to do with you, my love.'

'Is that right?' Erris folded his arms. 'Well, if we're keeping secrets, then I'm not telling you mine...' He jammed his lips together, eyes twinkling.

'What secret?' She caught Melinda's eye, laughing because they'd blurted it out together.

Erris chuckled, his eyebrows lifting by degrees. 'I just got a call...'

'What call?' Melinda was advancing towards him, scrutinising his face.

'From Kesney...'

For half a beat Melinda's face stiffened and then her mouth fell open. 'What? Is she—?'

'Her water broke...'

'Ooh!' Melinda seemed to inflate, then she was collapsing into Erris's arms. For a moment they stood, crooning to one another, and then Melinda was stepping back, wiping her face with her hands, fidgeting with her hair and her blouse. 'We've got to go! My baby girl *needs* me.'

Emilie's stomach lurched. If Melinda and Erris left, it meant that *she* would be solely responsible for looking after Joel.

'You don't mind, Emilie…?' Melinda's eyes were glistening.

Oh, God! She couldn't refuse, she just couldn't, even if it meant *she* was going to have to wait on Joel at dinner, as well as cooking. She sucked in a breath, shaping it into a smile as she let it go. 'Of course I don't mind. I mean…*hello?* You're having a grandbaby!' She gave Melinda a mighty hug, then turned her around and propelled her towards Erris. 'Go! Right now! Just make sure you text me when the baby comes.' She smiled. 'I want to know if it's a boy or a girl.'

'I will.' Melinda's hand found hers, gave it a little squeeze 'Erris will be back in the morning. Until then, look after yourself…and look after Mr Larsson too.'

She managed to smile, even though the hot dinner plate was burning her fingers through the cloth. 'Here you are…your main course of grilled sea bass on a bed of crushed baby potatoes and creamed spinach with a mustard honey *jus* and a black pudding crumb.' She set the plate down smartly, covertly frisking her fingertips against her tunic.

'Thank you.' Joel's eyes met hers. 'It looks…
wonderful.'

'Can I top up your wine…?' Even to her own
ears she sounded tentative. This was beyond
awkward. She was *not* a sommelier, she was
not a silver service waitress, she was a cook.
She could strip and slice an onion in seconds,
but for some reason placing a plate of food in
front of Joel Larsson was making her knees
tremble. The whole thing was feeling like a
silly charade. Fine dining for one! Linen, silver, crystal. It seemed excessive, especially
since he hadn't even dressed for dinner. He
was wearing a tee shirt and faded jeans, no
socks, and his loafers had definitely seen better days. He looked like a fish out of water and
she certainly felt like one.

He shook his head. 'No, I'm good…thank
you.'

'Okay.' She took a little step back. 'Enjoy.'

She walked towards the door, heart racing.
Were his eyes boring into her back or was it
just her overactive imagination? She had no
idea; two courses down and her senses were
shot to pieces.

In the kitchen, she took a ramekin of crème
brûlée from the fridge, then leaned over the
work surface. On the beach that afternoon
they'd had a few laughs, but from the moment

she'd approached him on the terrace to present
the menu, things had taken a different turn.
For some reason he'd seemed shocked to see
her, disappointed even, which had stung a bit.
When she'd explained that she wouldn't usually be cooking *and* serving the food, that it
was all because of Erris and Melinda's immi-
nent grandbaby, he'd seemed to rally. He'd even
smiled. But the smile hadn't quite touched his
eyes and, ever since then, she'd felt decidedly
out of sorts.

Out of sorts and full of self-doubt. She
wasn't convinced that he'd liked her starter:
hot smoked breast of pigeon on a bed of en-
dive and rocket leaves, garnished with a red
onion and beetroot jelly cube, and a port and
damson *jus*. He'd eaten it all, and three bread
rolls, but his face hadn't exactly been the picture of satisfaction when she'd gone in to lift
his plate, and when she'd presented him with
the main, he'd looked similarly neutral.

She stood up, rotating the tension out of her
shoulders. What was his problem? She'd got
top grades at catering college. Her training
with Michel Lefevre had been second to none
and at twenty-seven she'd started her own restaurant with Tom. She knew her way around
a kitchen better than anyone! She'd double-
checked her seasonings, taken great care not

to overdo any single flavour, or to over or undercook anything. She knew for certain that the dishes she'd presented were excellent…so why hadn't there been a single spark of joy in his eyes?

'Knock knock…?'

Joel?

She drew a slow breath and turned around.

He was standing in the doorway, holding his empty plate in one hand and the wine bottle in the other. His eyebrows twitched up. 'Can I come in?'

She felt her neck prickling, her mouth going dry and suddenly it wasn't Joel standing there, but Tom, his face taut, his eyes glittering…

'Two stars! Two bloody stars from Raoul Danson! I told you the menu was wrong, but you never listen! We're meant to be doing bistro food, not second-rate Lefevre! The restaurant's finished and it's all your fault!'

Second-rate Lefevre! Tom had certainly known how to twist the knife and now there was Joel, standing in the doorway. Was he about to do the same? She ran her tongue over her lower lip. 'Yes, of course. What can I do for you?'

He seemed to hesitate and then came forward, setting the plate and the bottle down on the island unit carefully. When he turned to her again, she felt a wash of relief. There was no reprimand in his gaze, just a trace of uncertainty. 'It's not about what you can do for me. It's about what *I* can do...' Blue-grey eyes held hers. 'I've come to apologise.'

Definitely not what she'd been expecting! She swallowed. 'For what?'

'For being—' his shoulders slid upwards '—weird.'

She jammed her tongue against her teeth. Staying silent seemed wise.

He motioned to the wine bottle, gave another little shrug. 'I was thinking...wondering if you'd join me for a glass of wine while I explain...' A corner of his mouth twitched up and it seemed to switch on a light in his eyes, a warm magnetic sort of light.

She glanced at the ramekin dish: a variation of Lefevre's famous pineapple crème brûlée. The sugar topping needed caramelising, but Joel didn't seem to be thinking about dessert, and anyway, she was curious. If talking was going to eliminate the awkwardness between them, then she was all for it. It would make the next three weeks easier.

'Okay.' She fetched two wine glasses from the dresser, then pulled out a stool and sat down.

He picked up the bottle, one eyebrow arching. 'Does *madame* wish to taste it?'

His fake French accent was excruciating, but it was good to see that lighter side of him again, the side she'd seen on the beach. She felt all her edges smoothing out, a real smile lifting her cheeks. 'No thank you. *Madame* wishes you to crack on!'

He laughed. 'Say no more.'

Laughing Joel was so different to serious Joel. Laughing Joel was dangerously disarming. She lowered her gaze, watching the red wine sloshing into her glass, then into his. His hand around the wine bottle looked manly. It was easy to imagine where that hand might fit, how that hand would feel—

'Cheers!' He was looking at her, glass raised.

She hadn't noticed him sit down. Too busy fantasising about manly hands. What was wrong with her? *Focus!* She touched her glass to his, took a long steadying sip, then met his gaze. 'So…?'

'So…' His teeth caught on his lower lip and then he sighed. 'Okay, the first thing I want to say is that I'm not weird, at least no more than anyone else, but I know I've probably seemed that way…?'

'Erm—'

'Never mind.' He smiled, took a sip of his wine, then his smile faded. 'So, the thing is, *I* didn't book this trip—it was a gift, from a friend.'

'Nice!'

'Yes, it was… It is! It's amazing.' His eyes clouded. 'But it's…not what I was expecting.'

Her heart dipped. 'What do you mean—is there something wrong…?'

'No!' He shook his head. 'It's my bad—totally. I didn't look at the brochure…just the front cover…the photo of the island…' He was toying with the stem of his glass. 'I thought I was going to be alone here so when you met me on the beach, I was—' he blew out a sigh '—very surprised.'

She felt a smile edging on to her lips. 'I think I got that…'

Amusement coloured his eyes, but only briefly. 'And when you said that you were the chef, I was, frankly, shocked…'

'Right!' She bit her lip, trying to make sense of it. His friend had booked the trip for him, but for some reason he hadn't read the brochure. *Why?* That was definitely weird. But it also explained a lot. 'So, just to be clear, when you say you were expecting to be alone, you mean alone as in Robinson Crusoe?'

He nodded slowly.

'You weren't expecting a chef?'

'No.'

'Okay…' She took a small sip of wine, felt a flicker of unease bursting into a flame. 'Are you trying to tell me that you don't want me to cook for you?'

His hands went up. 'No! I'm *definitely* not saying that.' He was frowning. 'I'm just trying to explain why I seem so…' He sighed. 'Look, Emilie, your food is delicious…and I'm not complaining about anything…but I thought I was going to be staying in a little house on a little island, doing my own thing, and instead it's—' he was juggling the air '—service and silverware and it's all too much. I don't want to be waited on. I'd rather things were more casual…' His eyes swept over the kitchen, then settled on her face. 'To be honest, if you'd be okay with it, I'd rather eat in here.'

She took another sip of wine. How would it feel with him sitting in the kitchen while she cooked? Weird, definitely, but there was something endearing about the way he was looking at her with hopeful eyes. If he'd been anticipating something low key, the house and the whole catering set-up must have been a shock. What would Melinda think?

She sipped her wine again, swallowing slowly. Probably Melinda was going to be too busy with Kesney and the new baby to care about where Joel wanted to take his meals… and there was nothing to say that he couldn't dine in the kitchen if that was what he wanted to do. *He* was the guest, after all, and, bottom line, her job was to look after him. It might even be nice. She smiled. 'I'm fine with that.' She put her glass down. 'Now, are you ready for dessert?'

'Have you been working here long…?' He'd have happily sat in silence, just watching her—the deft movement of her hands, firing up the blowtorch, adjusting the flame; the way the pristine sleeves of her chef's jacket rode up the golden skin of her wrists as she worked—but having asked to be there, he didn't want to make her to feel awkward by just gawping. Besides, he was curious about her.

'No. I arrived three weeks ago—from England.' Her eyes flicked up. 'It's just a short contract.'

'It's a long way to come for a short contract.'

Her cheeks coloured.

Skit! Somehow, he'd embarrassed her and he hadn't even meant to say it out loud. Giving voice to his thoughts was a bad habit, a side effect of constantly pitting his wits against computer security systems. For him, work involved an incessant internal dialogue. Talking himself through traps, fathoming logic, asking questions, answering them in his head—supposedly answering them in his head—but sometimes internal became external without him noticing. He'd have to be more careful.

She threw him a glance. 'It *was* a long way to come, but it was…timely.' She was moving the blowtorch back and forth, concentration furrowing her brow. 'I happened to be available and who wouldn't want a job on paradise island?' She held the flame away and peered at the little white dish which held his crème brûlée. 'The regular chef's on leave for eight weeks—a family bereavement, I think—so it all worked out.' She killed the flame and looked up. 'For me, I mean…not so much for the person who died…' Her lips twitched, then she was turning away, transporting the little dish to the fridge. He held in a smile.

When she turned to face him again, she seemed to have regained her composure. 'We'll have to wait a while now, for it to cool.' She shrugged. 'I'm a bit behind—'

'Which is my fault.' He tipped some more wine into their glasses. 'Come sit. You can tell me what you were doing before you arrived in paradise.'

She came over, but she didn't sit down. Instead she picked up her glass and leaned against the worktop. 'I think it's my turn to ask *you* a question…' Her eyebrow quirked up. 'Quid pro quo.'

Saying 'pro' and 'quo' had made her lips pout enticingly. He drew a steadying breath, reaching for his glass, then thought better of it. He was jetlagged, already a little muzzy and he couldn't allow himself to be muzzy. He leaned back, folding his arms. 'That's fair enough.'

She took a tiny sip from her glass. 'Why did your friend book this trip for you? And why didn't you read the brochure?'

'That's two questions.' And very direct questions at that, neither of which he wanted to answer. Her eyes were holding his, curious, expectant, but there was kindness in them too. He sighed. Nils was good at grand gestures and tequila shots, but he wasn't a heart-to-heart kind of guy and as for his own family... A knot tightened in his belly. That wouldn't be happening any time soon. Maybe telling Emilie, even just a little bit, would be a release. He unfolded his arms, sliding his glass over the counter so that it was out of easy reach, and then he met her gaze. 'My friend, Nils, who booked this for me, was *supposed* to have been my best man...'

Her eyes narrowed fractionally.

'The wedding was called off.' His throat went tight. 'Not by me...' He swallowed hard. That was enough; she didn't need to hear the whole tragic story.

Her eyes were glistening. 'I'm so sorry.'

Such ready empathy. *Undeserved!* He took a breath. 'That was eight weeks ago. These three weeks were supposed to have been our honeymoon…' Astrid had booked a honeymoon suite on Bora Bora, a luxurious overwater bungalow at the end of a long, curved jetty. He'd thought it looked romantic, but now the thought of it only led him into the same numb maze as always. He sighed, refocusing on Emilie's lovely face. 'Nils said that since I'd cleared my schedule anyway, I should take off, but I wasn't fit to organise anything, so he booked this for me, called it a "cancelled wedding" present. He drove me to the airport, gave me the brochure—'

'But you didn't have the heart to look at it.' Her eyes were lustrous, full of kindness.

'Something like that.' He looked down, suddenly unable to hold her gaze. There was too much honesty in it and for some reason it was making him feel like a fraud.

And then a little ping broke the moment into pieces.

Emilie shot him an apologetic look. 'That'll be Melinda…' She pulled a phone from her trouser pocket. 'I asked her to text me about Kesney's baby…' She tapped the screen, nibbling at her lip, scrolling, and when she looked up again her eyes were gleaming with tears. 'It's a boy! Seven pounds, twelve ounces. They're calling him Ben.'

His breath caught on an unexpected spike of emotion. What was wrong with him? Getting emotional about a baby wasn't his style at all. It had to be fatigue catching up with him. He needed to sleep. He slid himself off the stool. 'That's wonderful news! Please send Melinda and her family my congratulations.'

'I will!' She seemed to register that he was on his feet. 'Are you going? What about dessert?'

'You have it…' He smiled. 'I'm sorry, but I need to crash.'

'Oh! Yes! Of course. You must be exhausted.' Her eyes held his for a long moment. 'Goodnight, Joel. Sleep well.'

He nodded and turned towards the door. Maybe he would sleep well. If he did, it would be the first time in eight weeks.

CHAPTER THREE

'WHAT BIG EYES you've got, Grandma!' Emilie couldn't help giggling. 'You need to hold the phone further away from your face...'

'Wait a minute...' The picture wobbled, was briefly obscured by a pink splodge—a finger—and then Grandma's face came properly into view. Silver hair, silver-rimmed glasses, bright blue turtleneck sweater. She was peering at the screen, then she broke into a lovely smile. 'Emilie! I can see you!'

She smiled back. 'Who says the older generation can't grasp technology? You're nailing it, Grandma!'

'Isn't it clever?' More peering. 'It's like you're on television!'

'Smartphones *are* clever. That's why I was nagging you to get one, so we can see each other when we talk.' She stood up. 'It also means that I can give you a tour...' She tapped the screen, holding in a smile.

'Oh! What's that?'

'It's my lovely little sitting room… I've flipped the camera so you can see.' She panned the phone slowly, showing off the cream linen sofa and the gleaming wooden floor, and the full-length windows with their slatted blinds, then she walked through to the bedroom, showing off the bright sea views through the open French windows, and then, smiling because there was a lot of oohing and ahhing coming from the phone speaker, she entered her favourite space—the bathroom—tracking along the huge slipper bath, turning to take in the wide shower, and the square porcelain sink with its chunky chrome taps, and then it was time for the compact kitchen, panning over the wooden counters—

Grandma was laughing. 'I see Ruby in the fruit bowl!'

She grinned. Ruby was her treasured Rubik's cube. Grandma had given it her when she was little and she couldn't go anywhere without it. Crazy really since she'd never managed to solve it. She turned the camera back on herself. 'Of course I brought Ruby! She reminds me of you…colourful and chaotic!'

'Very funny!'

'So, what do you think of my pad in paradise?'

'It's lovely, darling! You must be thrilled

with it.' Grandma's head was bobbing up and down. 'Now, tell me, are you getting any time off yet?'

She nodded. 'Yes! There's only one person staying now.'

'One!'

'Yeah…' She felt her pulse speeding up. 'A Swedish guy. He got jilted by his fiancée, so obviously he's completely broken-hearted.'

'Oh, my word, poor man…but at least you've got something in common.' That was the thing about Grandma—no filter! 'Is he nice looking?'

'Yeah…quite…but he keeps to himself, more or less.' A splinter of hurt started aching in her chest. 'He gets his own breakfast, then he's out sailing all day, so there's no lunch for me to make. I'm only doing dinner… And Melinda's on Tortola with her daughter, who's just had a baby, so it's kind of quiet.'

Grandma's eyebrows arched over the rim of her glasses. 'And you don't like that, do you, Em?'

Grandma knew her all too well. She smiled. 'I'm fine, really. I've got lots to think about.' She pressed her teeth into her lower lip.

'Don't do that. You'll get lines around your mouth!'

She untucked her lip and smiled, widely.

'You know, peace and quiet is a scarce commodity these days. Have I told you about the little tea shop in Calderburgh?'

'No. You mean your favourite?'

Grandma scowled. 'It's not my favourite any more. They've modernised it! It's all laminate flooring and hard chairs, which are no use for stiff old bottoms like mine. They've stripped every bit of comfort out of it and the coffee machine screeches to high heaven so you can't hear yourself think, never mind speaking or hearing. I was in there with Audrey three days ago and we vowed never to go back.

'What the world needs is a bit of hush so if that's what you've got on that lovely island then you should make the most of it!' Her head turned sharply, and then the picture canted wildly before her face reappeared, bobbing in and out of frame because she was on the move. 'I've got to go, dear. That'll be Audrey at the door. She's dropping off a romance novel. One of those sexy ones. They're terrific!'

'Grandma!'

'Don't *Grandma* me! I may be old, but I'm still warm and breathing.'

She shook her head, smiling. 'Bye, Grandma. I love you—'

'Bye, dear.' And then the screen went black.

Grandma! What would she have done without her? When everything had fallen apart with

Tom, she'd instinctively fled to Calderburgh. Flying out to Abu Dhabi to stay with her parents hadn't even occurred to her. Their pristine condo suited them perfectly, but it wasn't home, whereas Grandma's house had always felt like a haven, a place where she'd felt at the centre of things, even more so after her grandfather had died. She'd always felt closer to Grandma than she had to her mum and dad.

She parked her phone and poured herself a cup of coffee, taking it out on to the little veranda that ran along the front of the cottage. There was a padded swing seat not far from the door—another favourite spot. She kicked off her flip flops and sat down, swinging her legs up. The seat stirred gently. Through the frangipani trees, she could see a turquoise ribbon of sea, could hear waves tumbling on to the beach. Paradise!

She closed her eyes, listening to the buzz of insects foraging in the nearby hibiscus and to the shrill chirrups of the yellow-breasted Bananaquits in the trees. Suddenly she noticed how springy the cushion felt beneath her and how utterly comfortable she felt. She sipped her coffee, savouring its rich praline notes. Good coffee, a comfy seat, tranquillity. If only she could bottle the feeling, take some back for Grandma.

'Is he nice looking?'

Joel on the beach…his eyes on hers…that dizzy, swoony feeling stirring her head around. Nice looking didn't come close, but she hadn't wanted to give Grandma any fuel for a fire. Melinda's teasing had been quite enough and it was all wide of the mark anyway. She needed a man like a hole in the head, and as for Joel…

She blew out a sigh. Four nights ago, when he'd come into the kitchen dangling the wine bottle, she'd been surprised, then she'd been surprised all over again when she'd heard what he had to say. Jilted at the altar, near enough! Sadness drained through her. That kind of hurt was bottomless. It was the hurt that kept on giving, the same kind of hurt she'd felt when Tom had told her about Rachel and about the baby they were expecting…

She shuddered, felt the familiar lump growing in her throat, but for once there were no tears to swallow, only snapshots flashing in front of her eyes. Tom and Rachel. Those little looks in the bistro kitchen, the way they'd squeezed past one another with trays as they'd gone back and forth through the doors.

She hadn't noticed it then, but she could see it now, the way Tom's face had seemed to brighten when Rachel came in; the way that Rachel had always come to work immaculately made-up: lip gloss, sweeping lashes, expensive scent. She could hear Tom's voice animating, Rachel's laughter tinkling. Only now, from a swing seat on the opposite side of the world, was she seeing what must have been going on under her nose for months and months. How could she have been so blind?

'The wedding was called off. Not by me...'

Grandma was right; she and Joel had a lot in common. They'd both had the rug snatched from beneath their feet. She knew Joel's pain, had felt its scratch tearing at her own skin, especially that first night in the kitchen when he'd been too upset to hold her gaze, but before that he'd been making her laugh with his bad French accent, and before that he'd made her laugh on the beach, and she'd felt that in spite of everything there was something nice happening between them...

The splinter in her chest twisted. But she must have been mistaken because although Joel had been perfectly polite since then, he'd also been distant, not lingering over dinner, not talking much. It had made her tense, made the atmosphere in the kitchen sticky and outside the kitchen...

She blew out a long sigh. Joel had been away from the house so much that if she hadn't known how much he loved sailing she might have thought he was avoiding her... She chewed her lip then stopped. She was doing it again, falling into the same old traps, finding new ways to make herself insecure! Of course Joel wasn't avoiding her. This wasn't about *her*! He was a broken man. If he was thinking about anyone, it was his ex…

Hadn't she been the same, over Tom? Shutting the world out, going over and over things…? That was Joel too, undoubtedly, wondering why his fiancée had called things off, or maybe he knew already and was trying to process it. Or maybe he was simply enjoying himself on the water, enjoying his surroundings and his solitude. It was exactly what Grandma had told *her* to do.

She sipped her coffee, watching a butterfly dancing a jig around the hibiscus flowers. Mindfulness! That was the thing. Living in the moment. Focusing on what was in front of you. Peace, quiet, comfort and coffee…

'They've stripped every bit of comfort out of it and the coffee machine screeches to high heaven so you can't hear yourself thinking, never mind speaking or hearing.'

She stared at her cup, realising suddenly that she was holding her breath. Grandma was spot on. Cafés had become noisy places and it was because of the hard floors and the hard seats, the wailing coffee machines. Surely there had to be a gap in the market for a different kind of café… A quiet café…

Café Hush—no, Hygge.

That was it! Café Hygge! A place which put good old-fashioned comfort first. Floors softened with rugs, seats with cushions comfy enough for stiff old bottoms. And the food… She swung her legs off the seat and stood up. Chocolate cake with thick ganache, gingerbread men, rich scones and—patisserie! Comfort food.

She felt her heart lifting. *This* could be her new business. Tom was going to buy her out of the bistro…that was what he'd said. There'd be enough seed money there to start something small, not in London, but maybe in Calderburgh! She smiled. That would give Grandma and Audrey somewhere nice to go.

She slid her feet into her flip flops. With Joel seemingly set on spending his days elsewhere, there was time to work on the idea. She could hone her patisserie skills and perfect some recipes for her old favourites. And if Joel did decide to show his face, then he'd be the perfect guinea pig, because if anyone needed comfort food, it was broken-hearted Joel.

Joel turned off the main road and jolted the open-top Jeep along the rough track that led to the car park—happily, deserted. He parked and jumped out, leaning in to grab his daysack. For a moment he paused, taking in the view. Blue sea and blue sky stretching away and, in between, the myriad humps of the twenty or so forested islands that made up the southern archipelago. This lookout point was the highest on Tortola. Ironic, seeing as at that moment he was feeling lower than he'd ever felt in his life.

He adjusted his sunglasses, shouldered his backpack, then set off along the path signposted to Apple Bay. It wasn't that he particularly wanted to see Apple Bay. What mattered was that it was a ten-kilometre hike. Walking there and back would make his muscles ache and feeling an ache in his muscles was preferable to feeling the different, equally insistent, ache that he was trying to ignore.

How had it come to this? Nils's gift should have been the perfect island escape, but for the past four days he'd been on the run, hell-bent on escaping from his island escape, fleeing from sparkling eyes, lips that lifted so readily into the sweetest smile and cheekbones that begged to be touched with a slow thumb. *Emilie!* He stopped to swipe at the perspiration breaking over his brow. *Kristus!* What was happening to him? Why were these feelings hounding him when, if things had gone to plan, he'd have already been three days into his honeymoon with Astrid?

He gritted his teeth. Bora Bora! He conjured the straw-roofed bungalow, the jetty, the turquoise water, but for some reason he couldn't conjure any anguish. He pushed harder, deeper. They'd have been snorkelling maybe…and then afterwards Astrid would have stretched out with her book and he'd have opened his laptop…and they'd have been peacefully absorbed until it was time for cocktails. He frowned, walking on. Aside from location, their honeymoon would have been an echo of their life in Stockholm. Steady. Comfortable. *Peaceful!*

The path sheared away suddenly, descending some thirty feet by way of steps cut crudely into the volcanic rock, then it flattened again, taking him into a stretch of dense forest. He pushed his sunglasses up and tramped along, brushing through fronds, taking in a million shades of dappled green, trying to spot the birds responsible for the shrieks and squawks he could hear. The air felt soft and damp against his face, and although the plants and the sounds were unfamiliar, something about the light reminded him of the forest on his family's island east of Stockholm. It was where he'd spent that first summer with Astrid…

He'd been sixteen. It was the year Astrid's

mother had been killed in a car crash. Her father, Karl, was his father's dearest friend as well as his business partner at Larsson Lüning Construction. Karl had needed support and time to process his loss, so he'd brought fifteen-year-old Astrid to spend the summer with Joel and his family on the island, except that Joel's whole family hadn't been there. His older brothers, Johan and Stephen, had gone travelling with their university friends.

Astrid hadn't wanted to hang out with his two younger sisters any more than he had, so increasingly they'd spent their days together and it had been fun because Astrid enjoyed the same things as him—sailing, exploring, building campfires on the beach—and although she'd been grieving for her mother and had sometimes taken herself off for an hour or two, the summer had been good...

He felt a gentle warmth filling his chest. That was how they'd started: two shy teenagers thrown together for a summer and becoming friends. The following summer Karl and Astrid came to the island again. That was the summer he'd noticed the way Astrid's body was changing, the way her large blue eyes held his. That was the summer they'd become boyfriend and girlfriend, the summer he'd felt his father Lars's eyes on him, felt a warning behind them…

'Don't hurt Karl's daughter…'

Hurting Astrid had been the last thing on his mind. He wasn't a player, never had been. He and Astrid had gone on, rock solid, all though university, never falling out, never hooking up with other people for fun like so many of their friends did. They'd seemed to fit. Maybe that was why, when he was twenty-two, Lars had taken him aside and handed him a small box containing the engagement ring that had belonged to his grandmother.

'You should make it official, son! Propose to Astrid at her twenty-first birthday party. It would mean a lot to Karl right now!'

Karl had been diagnosed with Parkinson's disease not long before. Maybe that was why Lars hadn't mentioned Astrid's happiness, or his own! He'd been thinking of his friend and had taken the rest for granted. A natural enough assumption! He and Astrid had been together for five years by that time. He'd accepted the ring, but he'd told Lars he'd rather propose in private. Hijacking Astrid's milestone birthday party hadn't seemed right, even for Karl's sake. It was a year later, on Astrid's twenty-second birthday, that he'd popped the question.

He stopped walking and rubbed at a glancing ache in one temple. Getting engaged must have been a joyful moment, but for some reason the only picture he could bring to mind was the selfie they'd taken straight afterwards. It was his laptop screensaver. A squawk shattered the thought. He looked up, saw a green parakeet sitting on a branch, attacking a red berry with its sharp grey beak. He watched it for a few moments, then walked on.

August was the time for lingonberries. He and Astrid had gone berry picking that first summer. He could see it so clearly...bright red handfuls landing in the basket by her feet. She'd smiled, said that when they got back to the house, she would make jam if there was enough sugar in the larder... He faltered, feeling a little dizzy. Jam, sugar, larder! Etched on his memory. Weird, remembering stuff like that! He walked on, picturing her younger face. Clear blue eyes. The dark green beanie she always wore... He faltered again, felt tightness banding around his chest. If he'd been happy for all the years that they were together, then why were his fondest memories of Astrid so firmly rooted in that first summer when they'd only been friends...?

He pushed the thought away, pushing himself faster. The track was twisting downwards now, becoming narrower and more overgrown—more challenging. But physical challenges were welcome. Thrashing his way through dangling branches and dense undergrowth was far easier than hacking through the thicket of confusion in his head.

And then the path exploded into a clearing and there was hot sun on his face and a ledge in front of him, overlooking a cove. A yacht was moored in the turquoise water. On deck, a man was lounging with a book in his hand and a woman was sunbathing. Two teenagers— boys—were jostling each other, then jumping off the side, all raucous laughter and splashing.

He parked himself on a boulder and stripped off his daysack, retrieving his water bottle. He gulped down a tepid mouthful, watching the family, his focus blurring. He'd grown up surrounded by noisy siblings, but he'd always been quiet. *The quiet one!* Johan and Stephen had joined Larsson Lüning straight from university, but he'd never wanted to follow, even though Lars had tried hard to persuade him. He'd always wanted to steer his own course. He drew an uncomfortable breath. It wasn't his fault that construction had never interested him. He'd always liked puzzles and strategy games so making a career in computer security had felt like a natural choice. And he was good at it. With his engagement to Astrid settled, he'd thrown himself into building his business, and now, eight years on, Larlock antivirus software was the number one brand across the globe. He was proud of that, but what had it cost him?

'Joel, we need to talk.'

She'd looked so pale and slender in grey cashmere, her silky, blonde hair twisted up, her eyes wide and anxious. He clamped his teeth together, swallowing hard. It can't have been easy, delivering the death blow. On the receiving end, it had felt like plunging into snow after a sauna: cold shock, disorientation, breathlessness.

He simply hadn't seen it coming. Yes, she'd been working unusually late for the past six months, but taking her place on the Board at Larsson Lüning when Karl's Parkinson's had made it impossible for him to carry on had been a huge adjustment. As Karl's only child, it had always been on the cards that she'd step up, but they hadn't thought it would happen when it did. There was so much to learn, she'd told him, and Johan had been such a help.

He closed his eyes, tightening his grip on the water bottle. Astrid said that nothing had actually happened between them, but that her feelings for Johan were real, growing stronger, so she couldn't possibly marry *him*. It was all so clean and tidy. A clinical finale. And now, after that initial, devastating shock, he was marooned in the numb fortress of his own skin, waiting for…what? Some stabbing pain to finish him off…to free him.

He sighed, swigging back another tepid mouthful. *Emilie!* She made him feel the opposite of numb, but giving that feeling room to grow would only set him more adrift. He didn't even know what the feeling was. Lust, desire… rebound stuff, definitely! He couldn't indulge it or let it show any more than he could tell her that he always left her kitchen feeling hungry.

The obvious pride she took in her work— the beautiful presentation of the tiny, delicious morsels she served him in the evenings—he couldn't put a dent in that because he'd seen that first evening how important it was to her that he liked her food. He'd messed up that night with all his awkwardness. It was why he'd gone into the kitchen—to explain—but he hadn't had the courage to tell her that the portions were too small. He hadn't wanted to hurt her feelings, because her feelings had suddenly felt more important to him than his hunger. Then, somehow, he'd been telling her about the wedding that never was and there'd been such empathy in her eyes, as if she understood…

He rubbed a thumb over his lower lip. What was her life like? What trials had she gone through…? The way she'd blushed when he'd questioned her decision to cross the world for the sake of a short contract…and that thing she'd said about how it had been *timely… Timely?*

He capped his water bottle and shoved it back into his bag. Maybe it was time for him to get out of his own head and think about someone else for a change. Without him having to ask, Emilie had helped him with the sail; she'd welcomed him into her kitchen, listened to him with kindness. The very least he could do was to stop being so distant. Stop disappearing all the time! Maybe *she* was in need of a friend, someone to talk to. He wasn't in the best place emotionally, but he could try to be that person.

He levered himself off the boulder, slung the daysack over his shoulder and retraced his steps through the clearing to the track. Going left would take him to Apple Bay. Going right would take him back to the Jeep, the Jeep would take him to the marina where the catamaran was moored and the catamaran would take him back to Buck Island…

He took a deep breath, adjusted his backpack, and turned right.

CHAPTER FOUR

'Emilie…?'

Her heart lurched and the bowl of sugar glaze slipped in her hands. She steadied it, breathing carefully, then looked up. Joel was standing by the dresser, perfect in a linen shirt and slouchy cargo shorts, his fingers resting on the radio's volume dial.

'I'm sorry for turning it down…' His shoulders slid upwards. 'I tried to get your attention, but the music was too loud…'

The clean, peppery scent of his cologne reached her on a ripple of air, speaking to her senses, skewing them. He must have been back for a while, showering and changing before ninja-ing his way into her kitchen. She swallowed hard. Why had he come? Why now, just when she'd decided to take advantage of his long absences! Just when she'd ramped up the volume of her favourite R 'n' B station and had been happily pottering with some ideas for Café Hygge! She wasn't even in her chef's whites. A clean apron over her vest and shorts had seemed perfectly reasonable for test baking, but now, for some reason, she felt like a rabbit caught in the headlights.

She put the bowl of glaze down. *Breathe!* Joel was a guest and he was welcome in the kitchen. As for her attire—she glanced at his battered loafers—he'd be the last person to judge her for being overly casual. She felt her pulse steadying, a momentary spark of gladness lifting her heart. It was good to see him—so good—but how was she supposed to react? He'd distanced himself for days, eating his evening meals with barely a word, as if they'd never sat talking over a glass of wine, as if they'd never laughed together on the beach.

She understood completely that he was heartbroken, probably so consumed with pain that he was blind to everything else—to *her* feelings—but facing him now, the hurt she'd felt at being shut out for days seemed to be sharpening itself, slashing tiny nicks in her heart. She wanted to be friendly, but she felt vulnerable, naked. The wounds Tom had inflicted still hurt and, whether he'd meant to or not, Joel had hurt her too. She couldn't lay herself on the slab again. She moistened her lips. 'It's okay. You don't have to apologise.'

She motioned to the radio, forcing out what she hoped was a friendly smile. 'I just wasn't expecting anyone.'

A dimple appeared in his left cheek. 'I can see that...'

Was he referring to the music, or to her baking outfit? His gaze was playful, and as for that dimple... *Impossible!* She pressed her palms together, trying to blow past it. 'Well, at least you didn't see me dancing.'

His eyebrows flickered.

Oh, God! She felt her cheeks flushing, her cool façade melting. 'You saw...?'

He seemed to hesitate and then he nodded, eyes twinkling, a second dimple appearing below the first.

He was clearly holding everything in, trying not to make her feel more embarrassed than she was feeling already, which was nice of him... But it was only dancing. Nothing to be embarrassed about, except maybe for the part when she'd been getting her groove on with the pull-out larder unit, but he might not have seen that...

Damn! Time to swing away. She took a breath. 'So... Do you ever dance?'

'God, no!' The smile he'd been holding in broke his face apart. 'Except when I'm drunk.' His hands raked the air. 'I don't have your...'

'Flair...?' In spite of herself, she felt a smile coming. 'Talent...? Rhythm...?'

He laughed. 'All of the above!'

He seemed different. Tanned, clear eyed, relaxed. It was nice to hear him laughing. Perhaps his holiday was doing him good, in spite of his heartache. If that were the case, she was glad, but it didn't explain why he'd come into the kitchen. It was way past lunchtime, and too early for afternoon tea. She felt her wariness seeping back.

He was moving, taking up a position at the other side of the island unit, leaning over to inspect the mini Bundt cakes she'd been glazing. His eyes lifted to hers. 'So, what's cooking?'

'Chocolate rum cake... I mean, cakes...' Needlessly, she nudged the bowl of glaze an inch along the worktop. 'Slightly different versions.'

'You're trying to choose the best one?' Mischievous smile. 'Let me know if you need any help with tasting...'

His gaze was warm and inviting, but she couldn't allow herself to dive in, no matter how much she wanted to. Tom had broken her heart, but Joel had stung her too, in a small way, and losing herself in his light, only to have him switch it off a second time, would be too much to bear. No matter how disarming he was, she needed to keep him at arm's length.

'I will.' She pressed her lips together. 'So, can I get you anything? A snack? Coffee? A cool drink?'

He straightened. 'Coffee would be great, but you're busy so *I'll* make it, and I'll make one for you too. Or maybe you'd prefer tea…?' He half closed one eye. 'At a stretch I could whip up an omelette if you're hungry!'

It was hard not to smile. He was turning on the charm, but he wasn't making coffee, or tea, or omelettes for that matter. She already felt guilty about him making his own breakfasts. 'Joel, you really *do* need to read that brochure. You're not supposed to be doing anything! *I'll* make the coffee. Can I bring it out to the terrace or to the pool…?'

His eyes fastened on hers. 'I was hoping to have it in here, with you, that is, if you don't mind?'

She could feel her heart straining at the leash, wanting to let him in, but if she did, what would happen this time? She swallowed hard. If only Melinda were there, to act as a buffer, but Melinda had organised time off to help Kesney with the baby.

'You *do* mind…?' The light was draining from his eyes.

She couldn't tell him she was wary of his mercurial ways. He was a guest. She nudged the bowl of glaze another pointless inch. 'Of course I don't mind... It's just that I'm busy.'

'No. That's not it.' His eyes narrowed. 'You're upset with me, aren't you?'

She bit her lips together. The nerve he was prodding was too raw.

He was shaking his head. 'The other evening, you gave me your time, your kindness, and I've repaid you with distance. Emilie, I'm sorry.'

The intensity of his gaze was turning her inside out. She felt her eyes prickling and looked down, swirling the glaze around in its bowl. 'It's all right, but I *really* do need to get on with—'

'It's not all right.' His voice was softening. 'Emilie, please. Let me make you a coffee.'

She looked up. 'Why?'

'Because small though it is, it would be *me* doing something for *you*, because if we have coffee together, then maybe we can pick up where we left off.' A smile touched his lips. 'Quid pro quo, remember? You asked me two questions the other night, which means you still owe me one.'

His gaze was tugging at her, but her insides were churning. She'd snatched at the threads of his friendship that first night because that was her way. It had always been her way, rushing in, bonding too quickly, too easily, because she didn't like being alone, but she had to change. She had to be smarter. Wiser. She had to put herself at the centre.

'Emilie…?' His smile was fading.

She drew in a careful breath. 'Joel, apologising is one thing, but we're not picking up anything until you tell me why you've barely spoken to me for days.'

His eyes clouded. He seemed to be wrestling with something, but she couldn't let herself feel bad for putting him on the spot. He needed to answer for his actions, not think that he could just smooth things over with a cup of coffee. And then he blinked, inhaled audibly. 'How to explain…?' He swallowed. 'Ever since Astrid broke things off, it's as if I've been dropped into a giant maze. I feel lost and numb. I can't see the big picture… I can't see how I fitted in, or how she did…or how we fitted together. It's like being in limbo…'

His gaze softened. 'But then, the other night when we were in here talking, I felt like I'd come back into the real world again. Everything was easy, *normal*. It was like breathing fresh air.' His teeth caught on his lower lip. 'But then the next morning, it struck me that if I hung around here, instead of excavating the last decade of my life, maybe finding some perspective and some closure, I'd be getting distracted by—'

'Normality…?'

His cheeks coloured slightly and then he nodded. 'When your world's been upended, *normal* is catnip…'

She felt the muscles in her face softening. She knew what limbo felt like. After Tom had broken the news about Rachel and the baby, hadn't she withdrawn into her own head too, hiding under her duvet for weeks—crying—trying to understand how the life she'd built had been torn to shreds? It was why *she'd* come to Buck Island, to escape the prison of her heartache over Tom, to get away from all that endless, miserable sifting through the past.

Being busy doing the job she loved, being challenged, was her *normal*—her catnip—and even though she hadn't consciously been thinking about Tom over the past three weeks, somehow, she *had* found perspective, had started seeing things about the past she hadn't been able to see before. Maybe Joel was beginning to see that avoiding normal wasn't the way out of the maze. 'So, you stayed away and now you've changed your mind… Now you want normal?'

'Yes!' His eyes filled with warm, soft light. 'But I also want a friend…and, more importantly, I want to *be* a friend, if you'll let me?'

She felt her heart tilting towards him, opening. Being friends with Joel was what she'd hoped for, but what if he stepped back again? It would hurt so much more next time, unless…unless she could harden herself, like her little conch. It would mean reining in that pathetic, needy side of herself that flowed out and wrapped itself around others so easily.

The problem was that something in Joel's eyes was already tugging at the soft, pink heart of her. He was a good man caught in a bad headspace, that was all, and if he'd had to retreat for a while, then it didn't make him a bad person. It made him a person who deserved a second chance, a person who deserved a friend…

'I have, haven't I?' He was shaking his head. 'You think I'll freeze on you again.'

'I don't…' *I don't know.* 'I'm just…'

She jammed her tongue against her teeth. Just that morning she'd had the idea for Café Hygge and for the first time in ages she'd felt happy and motivated. She'd made her little chocolate rum cakes, having wrestled with decisions about stem ginger and ground almonds, and then Joel had arrived. Now there were different, harder decisions to make, but thinking straight was impossible when his eyes were taking her apart, when just looking at him was making her pulse race. Friendship wasn't meant to do that. She bit her lip. If only she knew *how* to be friends with Joel.

He pressed his palms to the worktop. 'Emilie, if you'll let me, I can show you that you can trust me…' His eyes swept the kitchen, then fastened on hers again. 'But we'll need a change of scene. What do you say to getting out of here?'

She held his gaze. He was trying so hard to win her over. Hope in his eyes, but behind its light she could see his shadows. She recognised them because they were her shadows too. They'd both been knocked sideways; they'd both come to Buck Island to make sense of their pain and find hope for the future. Maybe that was enough of a seed from which to grow a friendship. If she made sure that the ties on her side were loose, then maybe it could work. She arched an eyebrow. 'To go where?'

'The beach!' A smile lit his eyes. 'It'll be fun—I promise.'

His smile was sunshine, irresistible. She felt its warmth surrounding her, burning off her lingering doubts like mist. 'Okay…but first, I need to finish what I'm doing.' She picked up the bowl of glaze, felt a smile coming as an idea popped into her head. 'I'll see you outside in ten minutes.'

'You're going to jump out of the way at the last minute.' She was twisting round, eyeing him suspiciously over one smooth, tanned shoulder. 'I can see it all over your face!'

He rolled his eyes, feigning impatience. 'Why would I do that? It would defeat the purpose. This is about trust, remember.' He steadied his feet in the soft sand, gesturing for her to turn her back to him.

'But that's the problem…' Her eyes narrowed. 'You've got this mischievous glint going on—' her hands spun the air around '—and it's not exactly inspiring confidence.'

'There's no glint of any kind; you're imagining it.' Except she wasn't. She was misinterpreting it, that was all. He knew that his eyes must have been shining like Christmas because inside he felt fit to burst. After four days of sailing solo and roaming Tortola by himself, being with Emilie, enjoying her company—just being normal—was giving him an abnormal high. Containing it was hard, but he'd have to try, or he'd scare her away, and since she'd taken some persuading to give him another chance, the last thing he wanted to do was blow it. He gave her a mock-stern look. 'Emilie, please, just turn around so we can do this…'

'Okay. Fine!' She turned her back on him, shaking out her ponytail, squaring her lovely shoulders. 'I'll do it, but if you drop me, you'll be sorry.'

Her playful tone was a dead giveaway! She was enjoying herself as much as he was.

'I'll catch you; I promise.' He settled his feet again, smiling.' On the count of three, just fall backwards.'

'Should I hold my arms out, like Kate in *Titanic*?'

It was impossible not to smile. 'If you want.' Out her arms went, smooth and toned. There was the sweetest whisper of a bicep. He felt an urge to trail kisses along her arms, then shook himself, clearing his throat. 'Okay, are you ready?'

She was giggling. 'As I'll ever be.'

'Okay! One… Two… Thr—' And then, in the next moment, she was in his arms, upside down, head tipped back, laughing, her eyes sparkling.

'You caught me!'

'Of course I did…' She smelt of spring flowers and spun sugar. Her bare arms felt warm through the fabric of his shirt. If he'd been wearing a tee shirt, they'd have been skin to skin. Just thinking about it made his breath catch.

'So…' her voice was a near gasp '…is this prolonged hold part of the exercise, or do you just enjoy looking up my nose?'

He smiled into her upside-down face. 'I was just making sure that you believe me now, that you know you *can* trust me.' He'd also been lost in the view, eyes, lips, and nose, but he couldn't tell her that. He gathered himself, then launched her upright, steadying her as she found her balance. 'You did well!'

Her eyebrows lifted. 'I did well to trust you?'

'No.' He shook his head. She was running circles around him, teasing, but he didn't mind. It felt nice, *normal.* 'You know I didn't mean it like that. What I meant was that you're brave…'

'Bravery has nothing to do with it.' She tidied her ponytail, fingers raking at the loose strands falling around her face. 'I knew you'd catch me because I'm the chef and no doubt you'll be wanting dinner tonight?'

Another round of tiny, delicious, complicated morsels. Not his idea of dinner, but he'd sworn himself to secrecy. 'You make a good point, although, honestly—' he clapped his hand to his heart '—it was the last thing on my mind.'

'Well, if we're being honest, then you should know that I don't really need trust-building exercises...' A scrawl of pain surfaced in her eyes. 'My problem is that I tend to trust people too easily, attach myself—' Her lips pinched together and then she swallowed. 'But I'm working on changing that...'

'Don't!'

Her eyes narrowed. 'What...?'

His throat went tight. He must have said it out loud. It was supposed to have stayed in his head, gagged, and bound... *Emilie, please don't change. You're perfect just the way you are.* He couldn't tell her that, but he had to say something because she was looking at him, waiting for an answer. And then a loud buzz filled his ear as an insect winged past.

Insect! He lifted his hands slowly and took a small step towards her. 'Don't move...' Another step. 'Stay very still.' Bemused eyes held his as he extended one hand towards her shoulder and swatted away an imaginary insect, and then he stepped back, pouring everything he had into looking deadly serious. 'Woolly wall bee...it's got a sting... You can't be too careful.' He swallowed, thanking his lucky stars for the local wildlife guide he'd been perusing just that morning.

'Woolly wall bee…?' Her eyebrows flickered faintly. 'Okay…well, thanks for saving me.'

Was she on to him? Maybe? *Probably!* He reached a hand to the back of his neck to hide a smile. Eyes full of sparkles and frowns, a smile as warm as sunshine. How could she think of changing? From the moment he'd spied her through the kitchen door, singing into a wooden spoon, snaking her hips around the larder unit, he'd known that abandoning his hike to Apple Bay had been the right thing to do. Dancing around the kitchen, she'd seemed so full of light and life that he hadn't been able to move. He'd watched her drizzling liquid over her little cakes…

And then he'd remembered that he'd come back to talk to her—to be a friend to her, not to spy on her—so he'd opened the door, calling out her name, but the music had drowned him out, so he'd turned it down. And instantly he'd been faced with the myriad shades of her confusion—the openness and then the wariness in her smile; the warmth and then the hesitation and then the hurt in her eyes—and he'd realised just what he'd done.

For days he hadn't allowed himself to take in

the details of her face because he'd been scared that if he looked into her eyes for too long he'd lose himself inside them, that all the things he'd been trying not to feel...that ache of the soul, that raw yearning...would blaze a trail through his veins and undo him completely.

So he'd shut her out, because allowing himself to feel so alive when he was supposed to be aching for Astrid had felt so wrong, disrespectful somehow to the long past they'd shared. But his way of respecting the past had disrespected Emilie in the present and he had to put that right, even if being her friend was going to be a sweet torment.

'Hey...' Her voice was pulling him back gently. She was looking at him mischievously, arms wrapped around the canvas bag she'd brought with her. 'It's my turn now...quid pro quo...remember?'

He wanted her to say it again, in slow motion so he could watch her mouth, but that definitely wasn't something you could ask a friend to do. 'You want a turn?'

'Yes!' Her lips quirked. 'As it happens, I've got a little trust test of my own lined up for you.' Her eyes held his as she walked back a few paces, then dropped down on to the sand. 'Come! Sit with me.'

It was a relief to see her eyes sparkling again.

Hurting her was the last thing he'd meant to do and he would never do it again. Not for the world. He stepped forward and dropped down beside her.

'Now, I want you to stare at the sea while I get things ready.'

'Things?' He arched his eyebrow. 'I'm intrigued…'

'Good!' Her eyes widened a little. 'But you need to be intrigued facing the sea, okay. Don't look round.'

'Whatever you say.' He turned, looking out over the vast expanse of blue to the hazy green islands on the horizon. The sun felt warm on his skin. The breeze felt soft in his hair. He closed his eyes, listening to the sound of the waves, and to the restless, shuffling leaves of the palm trees and then he focused his attention on the curious rustlings happening beside him.

Her face had been a picture as she'd lured him to her side, not that he'd needed luring, because being by her side was exactly where he wanted to be. For good or bad, whether it was right or wrong to feel what he was feeling, at that moment he wouldn't have traded places with anyone in the world.

The rustling stopped, then he felt her warm hand on his shoulder. 'Still watching the sea?'

'Yes.'

He sensed her rising up on to her knees and then the pressure of her hand intensified. She was leaning in, her breath warming his ear. 'I want to blindfold you…if you're okay with that.'

His stomach clenched. Did she know what she was doing to him? 'Whatever it takes…' Keeping his voice level was an effort. 'This *is* about trust, after all, and I trust you.'

'But is that wise, I wonder?'

Her giggle filled his ears and then a smooth stretchy fabric—a buff, he guessed—was sliding over his head. He held his breath as she adjusted the fabric around his eyes because her fingertips were brushing his cheeks and his forehead, sending red hot darts into his belly and his crotch. And then her warmth retreated and her flowery, spun sugar smell was carried off on the breeze. He swallowed hard, listening, trying not to feel aroused by the pressure of the blindfold and by the tingling uncertainty of what was coming next.

Suddenly the sand jolted and her lovely scent was teasing his nostrils again. Her voice was coming from the front now. 'Are you ready?'

'Of course.' It didn't come out as boldly as he'd hoped.

'So now…' her voice dipped lower '…you need to open your mouth.'

Instinctively he pressed his lips together.

'You seem to have trrrust issues, Meester Larsson…'

Her sing-song fake Russian accent was salaciously threatening, like a Bond girl, and suddenly the irony had him chuckling hard. 'It was involuntary! I'm sorry! It won't happen again, see—?' He opened his mouth wide, pointing at it with little jabs of his fingers. 'Hyee!'

'I can't tell what you're saying—' her Russian accent was dissolving into a giggle '—but never mind. I'm sure your power of speech will return after this…'

And then, suddenly, his mouth was full of soft, velvety chocolate cake and he was getting a hit of sweet, syrupy rum…tasting a hint of something that might have been ginger… It was the cake she'd been test baking in the kitchen. He felt laughter vibrating in his belly. He'd offered to taste them all, hadn't he? And she'd set it up…set *him* up by adding a cheeky dollop of intrigue. He couldn't stop laughing… She'd reeled him in, got him going in more ways than one and it was pure genius.

He ripped off the blindfold, blinking into the light, blinking back tears of laughter. 'Emilie!' She was kneeling right in front of him, so close, smiling such a smile. It was all he could do not to throw his arms around her. 'You got me good! As for that cake, it's out of this world!'

Her cheeks coloured just a touch. 'You think so?'

'I *know* so!'

She smiled again, then her gaze fell to the canvas bag spread out on the sand. There were five small boxes laid out on it, their lids loosened and resting on top. 'Well…' her eyes flicked up '…that's a good start, but there are five more.'

'So, you think the one with the ground almonds is the best?' She was handing him a bottle of water, her eyes wide and serious.

'Probably…' He twisted off the cap, weighing it in his hand. 'The texture of that one was great…but then again, they were all great.'

She nodded, a blush touching her cheeks. 'But that one *is* the best, I agree.' She smiled. 'Thanks for being my guinea pig.'

'Any time.' He took a long pull from the water bottle, watching as she boxed up the remnants and packed them into her bag. The tasting had been fun, but there was no doubt that Emilie took her profession seriously. She'd watched him so intently as he'd tried each cake, measuring his reactions to every mouthful so carefully that once or twice he'd felt a rush that had had nothing to do with the sugar he was ingesting. She hadn't even explained why she'd made six different versions of the same cake. By his calculation, he was in credit on the quid pro quo front. He screwed the cap back on the bottle. 'So what's the story with the different cakes anyway?'

'It's just an idea…' She seemed to falter, then her eyes were on his, narrowing slightly. 'I *will* tell you, but not today.'

She might as well have written it in the sand. If he wanted answers, he'd have to stay close, stay friendly. His heart caved. So she wasn't trusting him so easily, after all… He sighed. It was exactly what he deserved after the way he'd behaved. He gathered himself and got to his feet, holding out a hand to help her up. 'Another day then…?'

Her eyes held his for a long second, then her hand slipped into his. He felt his pulse jump. No wonder! The air between them had felt charged from the moment she'd fallen backwards into his arms. It wasn't his imagination! He stepped back, tugging her up, but he must have tugged too hard, or maybe she slipped because suddenly, somehow, she was up against him, soft, and warm, and close, and he was drowning in her eyes, and the heavenly scent of flowers and spun sugar. A loose strand of her hair blew against his cheek and for a moment he lost himself in a fantasy of taking her mouth with his, tasting her lips, her skin…

'Oops!' She was pushing herself back and away, head down, breathless. 'Sorry…my foot…it got caught…'

He looked down. Sure enough, her foot was tangled in the strap of her bag. He stepped back, heart racing. 'Nothing to be sorry for. Are you okay?'

Her voice sounded husky. 'Yeah, I'm fine.' She was picking up the bag, looping the offending strap over her head. 'I should go.' Her eyes darted to his. 'Erris brought a nice big crab this morning. I need to…do something… with it.'

He could tell that she didn't want a ride-along, but that was fine. He felt it too, the need to take a moment.

She started along the beach and then she spun on her heel, calling back, 'Joel, I'm sorry about what just happened…' She threw him a little shrug, then she was off again, walking quickly towards the treeline.

I'm not sorry.

The sound of his own voice startled him. Tingling, he watched her walking away. Long brown legs, curvy hips, ponytail swinging. A knot hitched tight in his belly. Had he ever burned for Astrid the way he was burning now? When they were kids, maybe, when it had all been new, but lately... *No!*

He raked his teeth over his lip. A year ago—*no!*—two years ago, Astrid had stopped coming to the island. He'd felt disappointed because they'd always shared a love of sailing, but he hadn't pressed her, because pressuring people wasn't *his* way...it was his father's. He swallowed hard, searching the treeline. But if he'd never pressed Astrid to go, then equally, she'd never pressed him to stay. He'd thought that they were just being comfortably independent, but maybe that was when things had started to slide.

CHAPTER FIVE

'ERRIS! WAIT! PLEASE!'

Erris twisted round and then his hand went up. 'Emilie!'

Her heart leapt. It wasn't too late! She hurried along the jetty towards the motor launch, dress flying around her calves. Its silky caress felt nice. *Feminine!* It was how she wanted to feel. Chef's whites were practical, but they didn't fall far short of prison duds and today she wanted to feel like a woman: a free, *independent*, strong woman.

As she drew level with the boat, Erris met her with a bewildered smile. 'What are you doing here?'

'I was hoping for a lift.' She planted her hand on the rail, catching her breath. 'I want to go to Road Town. Not for provisions, just to…' *escape from Joel Larsson* '…to look around!' She switched on a bright smile. 'I feel like a nice *long* wander.'

Erris's eyebrows flickered. 'What about Mr Larsson's breakfast?'

She felt her senses swimming and gripped the rail tighter. It was wearing thin, the dizzy rush she felt every time she thought about Joel. The problem was, she couldn't stop thinking about him... His smiling, upside-down face after she'd fallen backwards into his arms... Pulling off the buff, laughing helplessly... The way he'd looked at her... And when she'd tripped and fallen against him, she'd felt—*oh, God!*—she'd felt such an overwhelming desire to stay there, to press closer, to lose herself in his deep warmth.

It was all because of that stupid blindfold! What had possessed her? It was supposed to have been a little surprise chocolate cake picnic, to get his opinion on the test bakes, but then she'd noticed her buff in her bag after the unquestionably fake insect incident—an incident she still needed to unpack—and she'd got the idea. It was only meant to have been a fun trust game to follow on from his, because they'd been laughing and everything had felt so easy and sparkly, but somehow, things had spiralled.

From the moment she'd slipped the blindfold over his eyes her little game had taken on an energy of its own, an electricity that had skewed everything. Later, when she'd been serving Joel dinner, he'd been warm and friendly. He'd kept catching her eye, trapping her in his gaze, and every time, she'd felt her insides trembling and had had to turn away, busying herself with some small pointless task. It was physical attraction, undeniably, but there was something else too, gathering momentum, muddling her thoughts, muddying her vision…

'Emilie…?'

Erris's face snapped back into focus. 'Sorry.' She blinked. 'You were asking about breakfast for Mr Larsson…' Erris wasn't on leave like Melinda, but he'd been back and forth so much since Ben's birth that she hadn't had a chance to bring him up to speed. 'It's fine. He gets his own breakfasts.'

Erris's brow furrowed. 'That's not—'

'I know, but he insists. He likes to get off early, sailing.' She pictured the glistening fruits she'd arranged on silver platters for the previous guests, the eggs Benedict, the smoked mackerel mousses, the blinis and the delicately skewered cherry tomatoes, then she pictured the neatly stacked debris Joel left behind: the crusty remnants of scrambled egg around the non-stick wok, the plate littered with toast crumbs, the jammy knife, and the coffee mug with its milky dregs. She shrugged. 'I don't think Mr Larsson's a breakfast buffet sort of person.'

Erris seemed to be weighing it up, then he smiled. 'Okay then, come on. We'd better get going or I'll be late for the girls.'

On board, with the boat sliding away from the jetty, she felt her pulse steadying. Catching Erris on his outward crossing to fetch the cleaners from Tortola had been a good idea. All night long details from the beach had shimmered in and out of focus: the buff going over Joel's eyes…her fingertips brushing his forehead and his cheeks… *Deliberately?* Tiny lines around his mouth…his lips…listening for his breath to hitch… *Listening?* By first light, she'd had enough, knew that she absolutely couldn't see him until she'd straightened her head out, so she'd flung on her dress and made a dash for the jetty.

She unzipped her tote, hunting for her sunglasses. She'd given Joel a second chance because she liked him and because she'd felt sorry for him, but his trust game had done something to her. Caught in his arms, she'd felt bright and alive for the first time in for ever. She'd lost herself inside his deep gaze full of warm light because she was a moth, hopeless around light. He'd made her feel happy, and a little bold, so she'd played her game, but it had gone too far, thrown her off course, so that now, even with her badly singed wings, she was rising again, clamouring for...what?

She felt a lump thickening in her throat. Intimacy? Love? She swallowed hard. After Tom, how could she even be thinking of it and, as for Joel, he was still struggling to gather up his thoughts about his ex. Neither of them was in any kind of shape for romance. She bit her lips together. The most they could ever share would be a holiday fling and *that* wasn't her style.

She found her sunglasses and slipped them on. Thinking it through calmly, it was simple enough. She was lonely and Joel was hot! Yes, she wanted to run her fingers down the inky line on his inner arm. She wanted to kiss his mouth and that dimple that creased his left cheek when he smiled, but it was just fantasy. Joel was a friend—barely that—and that's the way things had to stay. Loose ties!

She drew in a lungful of air, looking out across the glittering turquoise sea. There was Café Hygge to think about... She could see it in her mind's eye, but that wasn't to say that she'd thought of everything. According to Melinda, there were lots of cafés and bistros in Road Town. There were bound to be ideas, touches of inspiration that she could borrow.

She felt her veins thrumming. Having a mission for the day was good!

She got up, joining Erris at the wheel, raising her voice above the sound of the engine. 'So, how's your grandson?'

'Very little and very loud!' He beamed, his eyes widening. 'Melinda's got her hands full, but she's loving every minute, no matter what she says.' He chuckled. 'She's already planning a party.'

'A party?'

'Just family and friends...but there's a whole lotta those so it's going to be quite a carnival. She's set on a beach party at Boulder Cay so that Anton can put on a bit of a show with his crew. We've not quite settled on the day yet, but—' he smiled '—you're invited.'

'That's so kind.' She felt stupidly teary. It was so nice of them to include her. She *had* to give something back, offer something in return. She bit her lip. 'Maybe I could help with the food...?'

Erris gave her the side eye. 'No! You spend your life catering. Everyone'll be bringing something: it's how we do it.' He grinned. 'Sharing the work leaves more time for celebrating.'

'Then I'll bring something too...' Ideas were already unspooling in her head. *A cake!* An is-

land cake, with a beach…sugar palm trees…
and sea… A blue crib with a sugar baby and…
sugar stilt walkers in colourful costumes! She
put her hand on Erris's shoulder. 'How about
a cake—a nice big one!'

He beamed. 'Sounds good to me, although
Melinda specifically said you weren't to do
anything.'

She felt a little glow of mischief. 'We won't
tell Melinda then.' She smiled. 'It'll be a surprise!'

She stood at Road Town's main junction for
a moment, considering. The three streets in
front of her were narrow, the tarmac cracked
and broken, especially along the gutters. This
was early April, edging towards the end of
the dry season, but it was easy to imagine the
streets running with water and the palms bow-
ing and thrashing in hurricane winds. Here and
there, dotted between the low, brightly painted
clapboard properties and the tall, white houses
with their ornate balconies, were palm trees
bearing the scars of old storms, tatty brown
leaves dangling like the broken wings of birds.
A little below the level of the tallest palms, fat
telegraph poles spat out wires in all directions.
Not quite picture postcard!

She picked the middle street, walking slowly.

When her father had called to tell her that one of his oil industry colleagues needed a temporary chef for a private island residence he owned in the British Virgin Islands—a place he let out—and that the job was hers if she wanted it, she hadn't hesitated for a second.

Between booking flights and packing, she'd pored over online pictures of perfect beaches, leaning palm trees and pristine yachts anchored in turquoise water, losing herself in the fantasy of it, but those wires lacing the streets together were a reminder that fantasy was just a manipulation of the truth. In real life, whichever street you took, there were always telegraph poles spoiling the view, or inside, little disturbances of the spirit spoiling a mood, like the guilt that was clawing at her belly for leaving the island without checking first to see if Joel's catamaran had still been on the beach.

She drew an irritable breath. Why was she worrying? He'd probably taken off early as usual and, even if he hadn't, he was used to getting his own breakfast. She'd agreed to be his friend; she hadn't agreed to stay on Buck Island twenty-four-seven! She yanked up the shoulder strap of her tote and stepped out. She *needed* this day to herself, needed space and a change of scene! And it was nice, wasn't it, not to be shopping for provisions. It was good having time to look around.

She took out her phone and photographed a cute-looking restaurant with a red wooden sign and then took more pictures of houses with roofs and walls and window shutters painted in rainbow shades, to show Grandma.

She drifted through a craft market, catching smiles from hopeful vendors, fingering textiles and jewellery, but she couldn't decide on anything so she moved on, going into a cool, airy art gallery so hushed that she felt guilty for even moving because every time she did, the pale wooden floors creaked. If she'd have been with someone, it would have been something to laugh about, but on her own... She headed for the gift shop and bought some postcards.

Outside, the heat hit her hard. On Buck Island, the heat blew through on a breeze that never stopped, but here, it seemed to bounce off the buildings and off the pavements. She felt light-headed, felt her palms sweating, and then she remembered that she'd been in such a hurry to catch Erris that morning that she'd left without breakfast. No wonder she was dizzy! She needed something to eat and a nice cool drink.

She cut through a walkway to the middle street, retracing her steps until she came to the restaurant she'd photographed earlier. It was the red wooden sign that had caught her eye, the neat edges of the cream painted script which said: The Roost. She'd always had a thing about signage. It had to be inviting and this ticked all the boxes. She pushed the door open.

Inside, it seemed a little gloomy at first, but there was a ceiling fan going, wafting cool air around which felt like heaven. She stuffed her sunglasses into her tote and looked around, eyes adjusting. It was a narrow, whitewashed space, with exposed eaves and white beams which made it feel airy. In front of her was a long wooden counter and above it, on the wall behind, was a wide blackboard listing favourites and specials: chicken with rice; goat stew; flying fish sandwich; roast pork and plantains; spinach callaloo. Authentic! Tasty and filling. She felt her stomach rumbling.

'Hello.' A sweet-faced girl in a white blouse and red canvas apron was smiling at her. 'Are you sitting in, or taking away?'

'Sitting in, please.'

The girl picked up a menu from the counter. 'Okay. Please come.'

She followed the girl through a pair of doors and felt a thrill of happiness. In front of her was a charming outdoor dining area set out with glass-topped rattan tables shaded by cream canvas umbrellas. There were high blue walls all around and stone planters dotted here and there, bursting with lush greenery. It was completely lovely.

When she was seated, the girl handed her a tall slim menu, then poured her a glass of water from a jug clinking with ice cubes. 'Can I get you a cocktail, or a beer?'

'No, thanks. Water's fine.' She fanned her face with the menu. 'I'm feeling the heat!'

The girl was nodding. 'It sure is hot today, so you just take your time… I'll come back in a few minutes.'

She sipped her water, watching the girl threading her way back through the tables, then she looked down at the menu. There was an appealing etching of a chicken coop on the front of it, but the vibe here was colonial-slash-tropical, not remotely *hygge*. She sipped again, felt her spirits plummeting. Café Hygge was a dream, but could she make it a reality? Tom had agreed to buy her out of the bistro, but when would that be? He'd moved into a new place with Rachel—a bigger flat at a much higher rent—and of course Rachel would have to give up working soon…

Her breath caught on a shard of bright clear pain. Why was Rachel the one having a baby and not *her*? She'd been with Tom since she was seventeen. They'd trained together, lived and worked together, opened a restaurant together, but…they'd never talked about having a family. *Why?* She pressed her glass to her forehead, rolling its coolness back and forth. It was *her*. She'd always been a slave to work, chasing perfection, *chasing glory,* because…she squeezed her eyes shut, felt the blood pounding in her temples…because of Sunday morning rolls buttered with smiles, because making nice food was how she'd got her parents to notice her.

Food and love, love and food, simmering for years, reducing, thickening, congealing, until in her mind they were the same thing. Food had always been her ticket, but not with Tom. She'd thought he loved her for herself, thought that once they'd ironed out the wrinkles with the bistro, there'd be time for a life beyond the kitchen, but he'd betrayed her and her best friend had stolen the life that should have been hers.

She felt tears thickening in her throat, seeping from between her lashes. *She* wanted a baby…or two…maybe three and she wanted a home that was more than the crash pad she and Tom had shared. She wanted a home like Grandma's, a home filled with laughter and love, and the smell of fresh bread… But she was behind the curve now. Twenty-nine years old with nothing to show for it. All she had was a fantasy café.

She put her glass down, shuddering a little breath. If Café Hygge was going to be her baby, then it was going to be a difficult birth. She couldn't see herself forcing Tom to sell the bistro so that she could get her half of the money back. That would mean talking to him! It would mean being cool and business-like. She wasn't up to that, not yet, but she'd have to change, somehow. Find a way!

She looked up. The waitress was coming. She wiped her eyes quickly, scanning the menu. Chicken and rice. That would be filling and comforting, not as comforting as having someone to talk to, but she didn't want to trouble Melinda and Grandma would only worry. As for Joel…no. Just, *no*!

Joel sipped his water, staring at the chink of sunlight dancing on the table. He hadn't needed a menu. He'd been to The Roost often enough to know that the goat stew was his favourite. He liked the thick, rich gravy flavoured with cloves and the pile of potatoes and greens and fried plantains that came with it. Usually he'd have been ravenous by now even if he'd had breakfast, but although he could feel his belly churning, his hunger felt distant and unimportant. He took another sip from his glass, felt its ice chill burning his throat. Everything seemed to be going...what had Emilie called it... Pete Tong?

Emilie! He'd wanted to see her that morning, to make good on his promise that she could trust him. He'd wanted to show her that he was her friend, so instead of taking off early he'd stayed in his room, catching up with emails, then he'd showered and gone down, but in the kitchen he'd found two young women in blue tabards chattering away, wiping the counters.

They'd told him that Emilie was on Tortola, that she'd got off the boat as they'd been getting on and that she'd looked 'very pretty', as if she was going on a date. As soon as they'd said it, he'd felt a snap of disappointment, then something gnawing away at him, a miserable cocktail of hurt and anger. He'd tried taking it out on the power boat, throttling it hard, tearing up the ocean, but it was only when he'd been tying up at The Moorings Marina that he'd realised what the ugly, alien feeling was: *jealousy!*

He slugged back another mouthful of water. When Astrid had told him she was falling for

Johan, he'd felt a flash of something like it, pain like a lion's roar—deep and loud and rumbling—but it had fizzled out quickly and nothing had flooded in to fill the void. But this feeling was twitching on and on inside him like a flame in a draught and it was just as useless: not bright enough to throw any light, not hot enough to burn off the mist swirling in his head. Had Emilie met someone here…? She hadn't given him that impression, but then what did he know?

He put his glass down, harder than he'd meant to. He barely knew Emilie, but she'd put in him a tangle just the same. How was that even possible? He was *supposed* to be too wounded to walk, too broken to even think about…what? What *was* he thinking about? He closed his eyes, massaging his forehead. Her lips…on his, his on hers, warm, urgent… kissing.

When she'd stumbled against him on the beach, he'd wanted to pull her right in and kiss her and he'd seen something gathering in her eyes too, but then it had faded and she'd stepped back, flushed and flustered, static crackling awkwardly around them. Maybe that was why she'd called back that she was sorry, unless she'd been apologising for the blindfold, and the teasing way she'd touched him.

A tingle raced along his spine. Her warm fingertips, her voice, the way she'd stretched out all the little moments—it had felt deliberate—*naughty*—but he'd started it, hadn't he, by choosing a trust game that involved physical contact. Truth was, he'd *wanted* to hold her, to feel her falling into his arms. *Kristus!* From the moment he'd set eyes on her he'd wanted her, wanted her like he'd never wanted anyone before.

He picked up his glass, swirling the ice around. If only she'd let him defuse the bomb afterwards, allowed him to smooth things over with some banal conversation, maybe everything would be feeling different today, but while he ate her mouth-watering Caribbean Crab Cakes Benedict, she'd been bustling about with garnishes, only catching his eye and smiling now and again, so that in the end he'd decided to give her some space and try again in the morning. But she'd given him the slip.

'Goat stew!' The waitress was setting down his plate, laying down the three sizzling side dishes. 'Can I get you a beer?'

'No, I'm fine, thanks.' Drinking wasn't the answer! Besides, he'd hired the Jeep again. Driving around Tortola had seemed like a good idea since there was no one on Buck Island to keep him company. *Ironic!* When he'd first arrived on the island all he'd wanted was to be alone and now…

'Okay. Enjoy!' The girl turned away and his heart bounced. Emilie was gliding past, stunning in a silky dress the colour of café au lait. She was heading for the exit, bag in hand.

He shot to his feet, catching his head on the edge of umbrella. 'Emilie!'

She jerked as if a string had pulled tight. 'Joel!'

'What a nice surprise!' He fought off the umbrella, nearly knocking his glass over.

She stepped nearer, a smile hiding at the corners of her mouth. 'You should probably sit down before you do some real damage.'

He grinned, knew that it was a goofy kind of grin because his lips couldn't contain it. 'I was trying to get your attention.'

Her eyes filled with sparkles. 'You did.'

She looked lovely, perfectly dressed for a date. He swallowed, looking into the space over her shoulder for any sign of a male companion. 'So, are you leaving…?'

'No.' She gave her bag a jiggle. 'I was just going to freshen up before my lunch arrives.'

She'd said 'my lunch'. He felt a flicker of hope. 'Are you alone?'

She blinked quickly and then her gaze settled. 'Yes.'

There was that same scrawl of pain in her eyes he'd seen before and it got him right in the chest. He felt his jealousy withering, his lust sliding into the shadows. Something was hurting her and he wanted to know what it was. She had no real reason to trust him. She hadn't even trusted him enough to explain why she'd made six versions of the same cake. He'd have to do better, work harder, be the friend he'd promised to be. He smiled. 'Would you like to join me, or... I could join you, if you'd like...?'

'That's...' her tongue hovered for half a beat '...that would be lovely, thank you. I've got a nice corner table. Maybe the waitress could help you move your—' She threw a glance at his food.

'It's goat stew.'

'Right.' She smiled, clutching her bag. 'I'll be back in a minute.'

'Joel, can I ask you something?'

His stomach dipped. They'd been chatting while they ate. She was in Road Town on a whim, she said—sightseeing—because she hadn't had the opportunity before, but although she'd been smiling, telling him about an art gallery with a creaky floor, he'd had the feeling that something was bothering her.

She'd kept glancing at his disappearing stew and he'd noticed how her knife and fork had stilled every time he'd spooned another potato or fried plantain on to his plate. Maybe he'd been attacking his lunch with too much gusto, but he couldn't help that! He hadn't had any breakfast and, from the moment he'd discovered that Emilie was not on a date, his hunger had returned with a vengeance. He set his knife and fork down. 'Of course.'

A little notch appeared between her eyes. 'At the house, at dinner, am I...am I giving you enough to eat?'

His stomach flopped. The way she'd been watching him, vulnerability flickering behind her eyes. *Damn!* He should have twigged. Making his own breakfasts, having hearty lunches at The Roost, then topping up with some street food in the late afternoons before going back to Buck Island had meant he'd been able to pace himself over her delicious dinner morsels and appear satisfied. Maybe he should have 'fessed up before now, told her that her portions were too small, but he hadn't had the heart. He'd seen that first night how much she needed his delight, his approval, and even if he didn't quite understand it, he respected it, respected *her*. So he'd stuck to his workaround and kept his thoughts to himself.

But now he was in a jam. The restless spark of physical attraction he felt around her was a perpetual torment, but more than anything else he wanted to know who she was on the inside and that would never happen if he lied to her. If he wanted to get to know her properly, then he was going to have to push past some thorns, risk a few scratches. He took a careful breath. 'The truth is…no.'

The light faded from her eyes.

'But—' he held up a finger '—that's because I burn calories like crazy when I'm sailing.' Which was true and, if he laid it on thick, would soften the blow. 'Sailing a cat is super physical and I'm probably overdoing it, staying out too long because the sailing's so good here… I need a lot of fuel!'

She frowned. 'It's why you've been getting your own breakfast, isn't it?'

He nodded.

She was shaking her head. 'God, Joel, I'm so sorry… You should have told me.' She bit her lip. 'Why didn't you say anything?'

'I didn't want to hurt your feelings. You put so much of yourself into it and everything you make is perfect.'

Her eyes glazed, then she was looking down, staring into her lap.

He felt helpless. How could he make her see that it wasn't worth crying over? It wasn't as if he intended to leave a bad review. He wanted to wrap his arms around her, but this wasn't the time or the place. He moved his plate aside and slid his hand across the table. 'Hey, Em, really, it's no big deal.'

'But it is. It must be.' She looked up, eyes glistening. 'Don't you see? I'm obviously so damned uptight that you didn't even dare to bring it up, even though this is *your* holiday and it's costing you a fortune to be here.'

'You're not uptight, you're just a perfectionist.' Something was happening in her eyes. Maybe he could turn things around if he could just keep going. He moistened his lips. 'I mean, *six* versions of the same chocolate cake! That's dedication…and remember, it's not actually costing me anything to be here because—'

'Your friend.' She was biting her lip. 'I remember, but still, he wouldn't want you to be hungry.'

'That's true, but I won't tell him if you don't.'

The light was coming back into her eyes. 'Joel…why are you being so nice?'

Was she kidding? He smiled. 'Because I have no reason not to be and…' *deep breath*

'...because I've got a Jeep for the afternoon with an empty passenger seat and I was thinking that, *if* you're free, we could take a ride, enjoy the sunshine. Normal stuff.'

Warmth filled her eyes, spilling over so that it was filling him too, then her hand was sliding over his. 'Normal stuff sounds like catnip right now.'

CHAPTER SIX

JOEL WAS TILTING his head in her direction. 'Not much further!'

He hadn't told her where they were going and she didn't care. It was just nice to be with someone—*with him*—winding into the hills in an open-top Jeep, birling along under a blue sky with the sun in her eyes and her hair blowing. What a turnaround! She'd been feeling lower than low, then suddenly, somehow, there he'd been, in the same restaurant, tangling himself in the parasol, looking ridiculously pleased to see her.

Catnip!

She eyed him sideways. How different he was to the way he'd seemed on the beach that first day. Back then, he'd been cool, wary, pale lipped, but now he was all open smiles and chaotic breezy hair. She felt a little tingle of happiness. He was gorgeous, but more importantly, he was big-hearted. He'd kept quiet about her portion sizes because he hadn't wanted to hurt her feelings. He'd made light of it, but she felt bad all the same. He was a big guy. Athletic! If she'd stopped scrambling around on the ledge of her own insecurity for just one moment, if she'd summoned just one iota of emotional intelligence, she'd have understood why he'd always seemed a little underwhelmed with the plates she'd set in front of him.

She turned, watching trees blurring past, green slopes spinning by. When had she lost the ability to see past the tangled web of head and heart, and food and love? How easily Melinda had seen the reason behind that sudden impulse she'd had to make dinner rolls the day Joel arrived, a reason she was only seeing for herself now…

From the moment Joel had turned his cool gaze on her, she'd felt the tug of desire, but there'd been something else too. That lost look behind his eyes had stirred her heart, had made her want to reach out to him in the way she knew best—with heart food—warm, comforting dinner rolls. But when it came to dinner itself, she'd stuck doggedly to the Michel Lefevre script, serving Lefevre-sized portions because—she bit her lips together—because she was good at it; because it was what she was trained to do; because it was her safety net.

She closed her eyes. When she and Tom had opened Blythe's Bistro, the plan was for relaxed fine dining, but then Tom had changed the script. He'd decided they should be doing gastro-pub food. She'd felt angry. She hadn't left a Michelin-starred restaurant to spend her days making shepherd's pie; Tom could have done that himself! Even so, she'd tried to create dishes that worked for both of them, but after Raoul Danson's pathetic two-star write up in the *London Time* magazine, Tom had lost it, had started calling her dishes 'second-rate Lefevre'.

She felt tears burning behind her eyes. If she'd blindly buckled herself back into her Lefevre straitjacket, then maybe it was understandable. She'd compromised her integrity to make Tom happy and had lost him anyway...

Joel was braking. 'We're here!'

She opened her eyes, saw a blue wooden sign.

PELICAN RUM DISTILLERY
500 YARDS

She pushed up her sunglasses. 'A rum distillery?'

'You can taste four different blends here.' He was smiling, spinning the steering wheel smoothly in his hands as he turned off the main road and drove them through a pair of weathered wooden gates. 'I was thinking that you could choose the best one for your chocolate rum cake…'

She felt a prickle starting at the back of her neck. On the beach, she'd congratulated herself for not telling him the reason why she was testing recipes. She'd thought she was being strong by not opening up at the first sign of friendly interest, but now she felt small and ungracious. Joel was trying to be her friend, trying to win her trust with a sweet gesture when he didn't even know what he was trying to help her with.

She felt something inside herself breaking apart and warmth rushing in. Café Hygge was hardly a state secret. Even if talking about it led her into a painful place, then maybe that didn't matter. She felt a smile brimming in her cheeks. 'Joel, that's so nice of you, so thoughtful.'

'It's *normal!*' He grinned. 'For the Caribbean anyway. If we were in Sweden, we'd be tasting lingonberry *likör!*'

'*If we were in Sweden…*'

What was his life like there? It was hard to visualise Joel under grey Scandinavian skies when Caribbean sunshine was dancing across his face. She wound a finger into her hair. His eyes were hidden by his sunglasses, but his expression was lively, full of curiosity as he navigated the bumps in the track, his teeth snagging his lip every time he eased the Jeep through the potholes.

She bit her own lip. It was hard not to stare at his mouth; hard not to notice his broad shoulders shifting under his shirt as he steered. He was handsome and kind and funny, but all she knew about him was that his fiancée had ditched him—*why?*—and that his generous friend had bought him an island holiday… She felt a frown coming. *That* wasn't nearly enough to know about a man who had gone hungry to spare her feelings. Joel was a special person and suddenly she wanted to know all about him— sorrows, joys, history, dreams—everything!

The rush of her own curiosity made her heart thump. She looked up into the canopy, slow breathing, watching the sun splashing through the deep greens and limey fronds. She saw a flash of bright feathers, tuned in to the chuckles and clicks and shrieks of the birds, calling and answering. *Quid pro quo!*

She lowered her gaze. Even birds had conversations. It was *normal* to be curious about someone, *normal* to talk. It didn't have to mean anything. If she wanted to know more about Joel, all she had to do was ask him a question

to get the ball rolling—something mundane—
normal! She twisted in her seat. 'Joel…? What
is it you do?'

His sunglasses glinted. 'For a living?'

She nodded.

'I'm in internet security.'

'Oh.' Not her area of expertise. She smiled.
'In what way, exactly?'

'I design security systems.' The track was
opening into a roughly made car park, beyond
which was a loose collection of old, stone buildings. Joel swung the Jeep into a space and
turned off the engine. When he pushed up his
sunglasses, his eyes were twinkling. 'Or at least
I used to… I'm more of a CEO these days. My
company manufactures and supplies software
for business and also for home computing.' His
eyebrows flickered. 'If you have a computer,
you're probably familiar with my brand…'

She pictured her laptop, the red padlock icon
in the taskbar, and suddenly felt her mouth falling open. 'You're Larlock?'

He nodded.

'Larlock antivirus?'

He nodded again, a smile playing at the corners of his mouth.

'Seriously?' She unclipped her seatbelt so
she could breathe. '*You're* Larlock Internet
Security?'

'Yes.' The cute dimple in his left cheek was getting deeper. 'It doesn't get any less true the more times you ask me.'

She closed her mouth. Joel was the Larlock billionaire! It was the last thing she'd expected. His shirt was Sea Island cotton, probably designer, and his watch looked expensive, but when he'd told her that his friend had booked an island escape for him, she'd assumed that it was because he couldn't afford one and the state of his loafers hadn't dissuaded her. But Larlock Internet Security was *the* leading antivirus software. Off the top of her head, she couldn't even think of another brand.

He was smiling. 'Why are you so surprised…?'

She touched her chest, trying to steady her heart, but his gaze was warm and twinkly which was making it race all the more. She glanced into the footwell. 'I think it's because of your shoes…'

A shadow crossed his face, then he squinted at his feet, laughing roundly. 'I love my loafers. They're nice and comfy.'

Joel sipped, tasting his own lips for a moment and then his eyes snapped up. 'What do you think…?'

She felt the fiery liquid sliding down her throat, felt its slow burn spreading through her chest and then she fanned her face with her hands. 'Strong!' She stilled, holding his twinkling gaze as the buzz travelled all the way to her toes and to the tips of her fingers. Was it the rum that was making her senses swim, or was it the way he was looking at her? It was hard to tell, especially after four shots. She didn't have much of a head for spirits and daytime drinking was a killer. Thank God for the big lunch! Even so—she planted her hands on the ancient wooden bar—the room was spinning.

'Emilie, are you okay?' Somehow, he was behind her, his heat radiating through the fabric of her dress, his hands scorching her shoulders. *Emilie!* She liked the way her name sounded on his lips and she liked the way his hands felt, firm but gentle. *Big hands!* The kind of hands she wished would go a-roaming. She felt a giggle vibrating in her belly. What would he do if she swayed backwards a little? He'd catch her, of course, because he'd caught her on the beach…his upside-down face, his lips parted, that tangle of fair hair falling into his eyes because it was long on top. He'd been wearing a different shirt, but the same cologne, and it had given her a little head rush then too—

'Emilie…?'

A shelf came into focus, then a line of dark bottles with bright labels, then more shelves, more bottles, then grey stone walls and then, with a little twist of her head, a pair of concerned blue-grey eyes. 'I'm here! I mean, I'm fine.' She wanted to giggle because he looked so serious, but she bit it back, trying to sound like a rum *aficionado*. 'I liked the spicy flavour of that last one. To my palate, it was the best!'

'Right.' His hands tightened on her shoulders, ever so slightly. 'Are you okay, though? You're not about to fall over?'

The giggle in her belly fizzled out. His concern was disarming and suddenly it wasn't the rum that was making her light-headed. It was his eyes, his heat, his proximity. She swallowed hard. 'I'm fine. Thank you.'

His grip slackened and then he was stepping back. A moment later he was leaning against the bar again. 'I liked that last one too.' He smiled, mischief flaring in his eyes. 'I'll get you a bottle, strictly for culinary purposes, if you tell me what the story is with those cakes you fed me on the beach…'

She felt her cheeks flushing, her veins prickling with residual static from her silly game. Did he have to have put it quite like that? She held in a smile. Of course he did! She'd teased him on the beach and now he was teasing her back, quid pro quo. It seemed to be their thing! She ran a finger around the rim of her glass, steadying herself. 'I've got an idea for a café: a quiet café specialising in comfort. Comfort *food* and actual, physical comfort.'

A corner of his mouth twitched up. 'Sounds like my kind of place!'

For some reason, his approval made her heart glow. She smiled. 'It was my grandmother who gave me the idea. She hates noise and hard chairs.'

'She's not the only one!' He was shaking his head. 'Those coffee machines in Roasta Coffee literally screech. I feel sorry for the baristas!'

'Me too.' He was *so* on the same page! 'There's nothing to dampen the sound so it's not even great for the customers. It's hard to hear what anyone's saying, so then you have to shout and that makes everything even noisier!' She moistened her lips. 'I think there's a gap in the market for a something different.'

His cute dimple was creasing again. 'So you're going to open a peaceful café with rugs on the floor and chocolate cake on the menu, and you're trying to find the best recipes because you like everything to be perfect?'

'Exactly!'

He leaned in, one eyebrow arching. 'And are you planning to blindfold your customers?'

He was milking it to the last drop, but she couldn't not to smile. 'I *did* apologise…'

'There was no need...' His gaze was gently searching.

Suddenly the air felt too thin. She looked away, gazing around the strange little bar which wasn't really a bar at all. Just a room with old stone walls and shelves for the different shades of rum. Before the tasting, they'd taken the distillery tour. As the guide had shown them the furnace and talked them through the process of rum making, she'd found it impossible to stop her eyes from straying to Joel's face, and he'd seemed to catch her every time, rewarding her with a twitch of the dimple in his left cheek, and then she'd smiled, feeling warm all over.

And when she'd been examining a stick of sugar cane and had passed it to him, his fingers had shaved so close to hers that she'd felt her breath catch. All through the tour, they'd exchanged little looks and little smiles. It had felt like being seventeen again, flirting with Tom in the college kitchen, reaching for a bowl at the same time, laughing at everything, things which weren't even funny. She'd forgotten what it felt like...

'Hey!' Joel was nudging her hands with a wrapped bottle. 'One bottle of spicy rum. Hopefully, it'll go down a storm at the peaceful café.'

'Thanks.' She smiled, burying the thought she'd just had and pulling another one on top of it. 'But the café's a long way away. It might never happen at all…' Especially if she didn't pursue Tom for the money. She pushed that thought away too. 'I was just, you know, playing with the recipes.'

He seemed to hesitate and then his gaze turned blue and clear. 'Emilie, I have so many questions, things I want to know about you and about your life. Is that weird?'

He was inviting her to step on to a bridge, not by flirting and teasing, but with a direct, open gaze. In her mind, she leapt, gliding over the bridge, and it felt warm on his side. It felt like a place she wanted to be. She swallowed, heart trembling. 'No, it's not weird, or if it is, then I'm weird too because I've been thinking the same thing, about you.' She felt warmth rushing into her cheeks, but it didn't matter because there was a new kind of light shining in his eyes, a light that seemed to say that they were the same. She shrugged a little. 'I think maybe it's normal.'

His gaze held her for a long moment. 'Do you feel like walking off the rum?'

She nodded, feeling as though she was answering a different question. 'Yeah.'

CHAPTER SEVEN

'So you got on a plane and came to Buck Island…' He levered up a low branch so that Emilie could pass underneath. For some reason, the delicate floral scent that lingered in her wake was fuelling the fierce ache he was feeling in his chest. How could her partner have cheated on her like that, with her best friend, right under her nose, effectively forcing her out of her own bistro? No one deserved that, especially not someone as kind and lovely as Emilie. He felt a stab of guilt. That quip he'd made about the short contract—no wonder she'd looked so uncomfortable—he'd just stirred her pain around. If only he'd kept his big mouth shut!

'It was a no-brainer.' She was walking slowly, waiting for him to catch up. 'There was nothing to keep me in England. The job gave me an excuse to run away. I wanted to be too busy to think about things.'

He felt another twinge in his chest. 'And I messed everything up. The solitary guest who didn't even want you to make his breakfast. I'm so sorry.'

'No, *I'm* sorry.' She stopped walking. 'If I'd been paying attention, I'd have put two and two together right away, seen that you were a full English kind of guy…' She tilted her head. 'Do you understand what that means?'

He felt his mood lifting. 'Bacon, eggs, sausage, mushrooms, grilled tomato, fried bread….' Her eyes were widening comically. He laughed. 'My mother's half-English.'

'Ahh!' She was giving him snake eyes. 'That explains the scrambled egg and toast.'

'You're a food detective!'

'I might be good with evidence, but I need to hone my intuition.'

'Hey! We squared it away.' Why did she take so much on to herself? He nudged her shoulder. 'Stop beating yourself up.'

She shot him a little smile then carried on walking. 'So, two older brothers and two younger sisters…?' He'd given her a brief anatomy of his family after she'd told him about her sisters—older, and twins—and her parents, who were living in Abu Dhabi. 'What was that like?'

'Hell on earth.'

'You're joking, right…?' She was looking at him suspiciously.

Was he joking? Suddenly, he felt uncomfortable. He'd never had to answer a question like this before. Astrid had been a part of his family for so long that he'd never had to articulate his feelings to her.

When he was growing up, he'd mostly thought about escaping, about getting away from the non-stop clattering of feet on the stairs, from the clamouring voices over dinner as dishes were passed hand to hand, from all the bright-eyed teasing and the endless bragging, and from his father, Lars, the hub of the wheel, stirring it round, over-winding it like a clock. Did he want to get into all that with Emilie? *No!* He reached a hand to the back of his neck, mustering a smile. 'Of course I'm joking. It was noisy, too noisy at times, but it was fun.'

Her eyebrows flickered. 'You don't sound so enthusiastic.'

'Don't I?' He pictured sledging with Johan and Stefan, tumbling off, cold handfuls of snow being thrust down his back, the yelling, the jostling. He masked a shudder with a shrug. 'Look, I love my brothers and sisters.' *Johan…* 'They're good people, but I'm different to them. I'm the quiet one.'

She was smiling, warming him all the way through. 'You really *are* the perfect customer for my café!'

'You have no idea!' He pushed a large leaf aside for her. It felt nice talking to Emilie. *Easy!* 'My family owns an island north-east of Stockholm. When we were there, I used to go off sailing for hours.' He caught her eye. 'I'd take great big English-style sandwiches and a bottle of water. When I was tired, I'd stop, drop the sails and drift. It was heaven, floating on the sea by myself. I guess I've always been a lone wolf, wanting to do my own thing.' He felt a knot tightening in his stomach, a quick beat of indecision, then he pushed on. 'Much to my father's displeasure I didn't go into the family business.'

Emilie turned slightly. 'What's the family business?'

'Larsson Lüning Construction. Large-scale projects all over the world. I'm the only Larsson sibling who isn't on the Board—*my* choice.' Why was he doing this, emptying all the drawers?

She went quiet for a moment and then her eyes settled on his. 'But still, your father must be proud of you? I mean, *hello,* it's not like you haven't achieved anything.'

He swallowed hard, picturing his father's

smile, the way it always seemed to stop short. 'Lars likes success, so he *is* proud that I've done well, but he's disappointed in *me* because he thinks I haven't been loyal.'

Emilie was frowning. 'Your father thinks you're disloyal because you built your own business?'

'Lars likes to get his own way.' He felt a sour taste gathering at the back of his mouth. 'He's determined. Single-minded. He's probably just pissed that he's failed to bend my will to his, annoyed that I haven't put my shoulder to the Larsson Lüning wheel. I've probably injured his damn pride or something.' He could hear the bitterness on his voice, see Emilie's eyes growing wider. He needed to rein it in.

'You're determined too, though.' Her gaze was direct. 'I mean, going off like that, on your own, sailing all day, when you were how old...?'

He shrugged. 'I don't know, eight, nine, ten.'

She was shaking her head. 'I could *never* have done anything like that. Just the thought of it...being alone on the sea, for hours.' She shuddered. 'Maybe you and Lars are actually the same. Maybe *you* intimidate him—'

'No way!' His pulse was banging. 'My father is loud, pushy, bullish. He can be amusing at times, but—' he felt a shudder travelling up his spine '—I'm not like him. Not at all!'

'Except for being amusing at times...' She was arching an eyebrow, a gentle irresistible warmth in her eyes.

He felt his tension melting away, a smile tugging at his lips. How could she do that, bring him back with just one look?

They were coming out of the forest now, walking into a bright blaze of sunshine. He looked ahead, scanning the line of the path which ran upwards, climbing gradually through the cane fields to a lookout point. The distillery guide had said there was a café up there, a great view over the bay. He turned. 'Do you want to keep going?'

She was standing a few yards back, rooting around in her bag. 'I'd love to, but I'm worrying about the time.' She pulled out her phone. 'Erris is picking me up from the marina at four.'

'Oh!' It felt too soon. He liked being with her, just walking and talking, even about his family. *Lars.* It was liberating, letting off steam to someone who...his breath snagged on the thought...someone who had no connection. He ran his tongue over his lip. Maybe that was why the bitterness he hadn't fully known was there had seeped out. He blinked. And Emilie had been so gentle with him, so non-judgemental. He drew in a slow breath. She was squinting at her phone, silk billowing around her legs, bag hanging off her smooth bare shoulder. He felt heat flooding into his belly, into his groin.

All through the distillery tour he'd felt static shuttling between them. Every look, every smile. In the bar, it had taken all his willpower not to step in and pull her close. When he'd thought she was meeting someone, he'd burned with jealousy and now he was burning with longing, but what could really happen between them? A fling? No strings? That was all it could ever be because she was broken and vulnerable, and he was confused, still probing the numb black space inside himself, trying to find the bleeding wound that Astrid and Johan had inflicted.

He inhaled slowly, stepping back in his head. He wasn't a fling kind of guy, but at the same time, when Emilie had said she wanted to get to know him, he'd felt a spark of pure joy, a little upward boost as if an elevator had whipped him up a floor. And now he was on that floor, he wanted to stay, wanted *her* to stay. Would she? He moistened his lips. 'Come back with me…'

She looked up, smiling a thin smile. 'I wish I could, but unfortunately *this*—' she tugged at her dress '—is not a sailing outfit.'

Maybe fate was on his side after all. He grinned. 'I've got the powerboat today.'

'Oh!' Her eyes lit with a smile. 'How perfect is that? This dress loves a powerboat.'

A bubble of happiness exploded in his chest. 'Well, that settles it. What the dress wants, the dress gets.'

'Here! Let me help you…' Joel was on the jetty, holding out his hand. A smile hung about his lips, but his eyes looked cool. Maybe it was just the glow of twilight bouncing off the pale hull of the boat.

She shouldered her bag and slipped her hand into his. It felt warm and strong. *Dependable!* She leaned into it, letting him guide her out of the boat and then she smiled. 'I had a nice time today.'

'Me too.' His fingers flexed around hers and then he stepped back, busying himself with the mooring ropes.

She felt the air trickling from her lungs. He seemed preoccupied. Maybe he was like her, wondering how they were going to say good-night. She felt her belly trembling and turned, looking back across the sea to the winking lights on Tortola. If she'd come back with Erris there'd have been none of this awkwardness… but there'd have been none of the joy either, none of the soaring happiness she'd felt when Joel had said he'd got the powerboat.

After she'd phoned Erris, they'd walked to the café overlooking the bay, parking themselves outside, drinking iced tea, and then maybe because Joel had opened up a little bit about his family, she'd opened up too, filling in the thumbnail sketch she'd given him earlier, telling the full story of how Tom had persuaded her to leave Le Perroquet so they could strike out on their own and about how Rachel had stepped in to help. She'd told him how Tom had shifted the goalposts, about the scathing review and about how she'd tried to make things work, but she didn't tell him about Tom and Rachel's baby. That was too raw, too hard to talk about.

She'd hoped he'd tell her about Astrid in return, but on the walk back to the distillery he'd seemed intent on telling her about his youthful sailing escapades. He'd made her laugh, mimicking countless body blows from the swinging boom, but then guilt had started pooling around her ankles because she was supposed to have been on Buck Island, cooking for him. He'd picked up on her fretting, brushing her worries aside with a twinkly smile. He'd said there was a great street food place in Road Town she'd like—Clara's Kitchen—and that he wasn't taking no for an answer.

She'd more than liked it! Bare bulb strings

looped around the canopied dining area, the rustic tables, the sizzling platters, all the spicy, smoky aromas. And she'd loved the look on Joel's face, the glow of the sunset on his skin, the way his eyes had been shining. She felt her heart twisting slowly. The light in Joel's eyes pushed everything into the shadows, but Tom had dazzled her like that once, blinding her. She felt a dry edge in her throat. Had she been walking blind for all this time…? Something to think about, but this wasn't the time or the place.

She turned. Joel was bent to one of the mooring posts, tying off a rope, tugging it tight. Did he feel trapped in awkwardness too, or were her own jitters skewing her intuition? It had been a long day, tiring. No wonder her edges were blurring. She took a step. 'Joel, it's getting late. I'm going to go…'

He straightened. 'I'll walk you.'

'Oh!' Her heart dipped. That would only be postponing the goodnight bit. 'That's very chivalrous of you but, really, there's no need. It's a two-minute walk—'

He smiled. 'I think I can spare two minutes.'

'Oh, okay.' She smiled back. 'Thanks.' She started along the jetty, butterflies raging in her belly as he fell in beside her. With every in-breath she could smell the faint musk of his cologne, could feel it spiralling through her veins. They should have come back before the light had started fading, then things wouldn't have felt quite so…loaded. She glanced at him. He seemed preoccupied again. She needed to say something—*anything*—to break the silence. She licked her lips. 'It's a long time since anyone walked me home.'

Something flickered behind his eyes. 'It's a long time since I *walked* anyone home.'

Oh, God! Had he used to walk Astrid home? Was he thinking about Astrid at that very moment? Maybe that was why he was subdued. She glanced at him again. His jaw looked tight, his mouth firm, as though he was biting on a bullet. If he'd opened up to her about Astrid, then she'd have been better equipped…but now wasn't the right time for asking.

She looked ahead. The small solar lights which edged the forest path were crawling with moths and tiny bugs, and the air was alive with the chirrups and the sleepy calls of roosting birds. When the breeze rippled, a burst of heady scent filled her nostrils. She heard Joel breathing it in. She smiled. 'It's lovely, isn't it?'

'Yes, it is.' He blinked and then his gaze settled. 'What is it?'

'It's the Jamaican Caper.' There was a bush at the side of the path. She went to it, pointing

out the white flowers, the sprays of long sta-
mens. 'See, it blooms at night.'

His lips twitched. 'It looks like a sparkler.'

'It does!' She smiled. 'It's so beautiful.'

'It *is* beautiful.' Her heart thumped. He
wasn't looking at the flowers. His eyes were
fastened on hers. He swallowed slowly. 'It's the
most beautiful thing I've ever seen...'

What was he saying? She felt the path tilting, a rush of dizziness. His cologne was in her
lungs and his gaze was soft...hypnotic... She
was drifting, looking at his mouth, wanting...
No! She turned away, glimpsed pale clapboard
through the trees. 'Look!' Somehow, her feet
were moving, carrying her quickly and then
she was dashing on, calling back, 'We're here.'

At the cottage door she stopped, heart drumming. What was she running from? That fond,
magnetic light in his eyes or her own fear? Fear
of being blinded again, scared of getting caught
in a rip tide, of being dragged under and dashed
on the rocks... Joel had said she made him feel
normal, but what they'd been sharing all day
had overshot normal by miles. It had felt special. Joel had made her *feel* special: jumping to
his feet at The Roost with delighted eyes; lining
up the rums for her to taste at the distillery; listening so attentively as she'd talked about food
and flavours at Clara's Kitchen...

She dropped her bag, then leaned, pressing her forehead to the door, guilt curling in her toes. She hadn't had to cook anything to get Joel's attention. He'd made her feel important, wanted, for simply being herself. Then, gentleman that he was, he'd insisted on walking her home and what had she done? Left him on the path feeling…what? Bewildered? Hurt? She felt tears stinging her eyes. It was all Tom's fault. *He'd* made her like this, not Joel. Joel had treated her like a precious thing. For all she knew, getting closer to Joel might actually be the cure, the way to push Tom's hurt into the shadows, but it was too late now. He was probably already striding back to the house—

'Emilie.'

Joel! She felt a sob struggling up her throat, tears sliding down her cheeks. She'd run and he'd come after her. She couldn't turn round for shame.

'Emilie…' The deck creaked under his footstep and then his warmth filled the space behind her. 'What's wrong?' His voice was gentle, close. 'Have I upset you?'

Air funnelled into her lungs at breakneck speed. How could he even think such a thing? She spun round, wiping her face. 'No! It's not you…'

'But you're crying.' His eyes were searching, taking her apart, then his hands came up and he was brushing her wet cheeks with the backs of his knuckles. 'Why?'

Her belly quivered. Had Tom ever touched her as tenderly as this? She couldn't remember, couldn't remember ever feeling so weak, so full of longing. 'I'm crying because you gave me a lovely day and I left you on the path when you were about to...' The words dried on her tongue. Maybe she'd got it wrong, misread the whole thing. *Oh, God!*

His eyes narrowed. 'About to what?'

She felt her neck prickling. She couldn't not tell him the truth. 'I thought you were going to kiss me and I was scared because... I don't know...because of Tom...and because I'm not sure about anything any more.'

His hands fell from her face and then he swallowed. 'I was thinking about it, but I'm not sure either.' Something came and went behind his eyes. 'It's probably for the best.'

She pressed her lips together. Tom was the only man she'd ever been with and she'd never looked past him, but now something was unravelling, taking hold of her senses. What would it be like with Joel? How would it feel? She wanted to know, *needed* to know. She took a breath, resting her hands on his chest. 'Kiss me...'

His eyes darted to her mouth, a landscape of light and shade in his eyes. She slid her hands upwards, to the sides of his neck, and on until she was holding his face. 'I want you to.'

An animal noise rumbled in his throat and then his mouth was on hers. She closed her eyes, losing herself in the sweet caress of his lips, the stroke of his tongue, the hot, urgent exploring. She was being gathered in, crushed into the smooth hard planes of his body and it was too much to feel, too much to taste, too much, but at the same time it wasn't enough, not nearly enough.

'Emilie!' It was a ragged exclamation, then his eyes were on hers. She felt the warm pad of his thumb moving over her cheekbone, a fresh tug of desire drawing tight in her belly. 'Have you got any idea what you're doing to me...?'

She nodded. Her lips felt used, swollen, still hungry. 'I do because you're doing it to me too.' She wound her fingers into his hair, pulling him in, and for a moment his lips took hers again, but then he was pulling away, stepping back.

'Wait!' He put his hands on her shoulders, holding her at a distance. His eyes were fire and ice. 'I can't... I'm not...' He was shaking his head. 'I'm sorry. I've got to go.' His fingers flexed, then his hands fell from her shoulders and he was going, down the veranda step, over the grass, heading back towards the path.

She touched her mouth, still reeling. She was missing him already, but if they'd carried on, they'd have been—what? Holiday lovers? She blinked. That would confuse things and confusion was the last thing either of them needed. Walking away was the right decision, even if it didn't feel right. At least this way, they could stay friends. He *needed* to know that they *were* still friends. She ran to the edge of the veranda. 'Joel!'

He half turned.

'It's okay.' She swallowed. 'I'll see you tomorrow…?'

He seemed to hesitate, then he threw up a hand and disappeared into the trees.

CHAPTER EIGHT

JOEL LOWERED HIMSELF on to the trampoline of the catamaran, rolling back so he could stare at the sky. Sailing was his jam—he always felt loose afterwards—but today, although the conditions had been perfect for flying the hull and he'd raced around the eastern side of Tortola with the sun and spray on his face, he was still wound tight.

He shifted, rolling his shoulders, stretching out his neck. *'Kiss me.'* That huskiness in her voice, that bright flame of desire in her eyes. All night, fragments from the veranda had been looping in his head. He couldn't get over the way Emilie had wanted him, the way it had felt, like firing on all cylinders, his senses exploding and imploding at the same time.

It was new. Raw. Powerful. *Too powerful.* He'd had to leave, *had to*, because hooking up for a night wasn't his style and he wasn't in any shape for a relationship. He was caught in the gap, no good for anything, but he couldn't forget the way she'd tasted, the heat in her mouth, the way her body had seemed to fuse with his. He drew in a long breath, trying to inhale some clarity. Why was he so tangled up? Emilie had shouted after him that it was 'okay', so why was he struggling to write off that kiss as a momentary loss of self-control? He was burning up with too many feelings, confusing feelings, and wasn't he already confused enough about Astrid?

Emilie! The day before he'd been twitching away at the thought of her being with someone else. That might have been a by-product of the tingling static that had been shuttling through his veins ever since she'd slipped that blindfold over his eyes. He could rationalise that desire had turned him into a hothead, a jealous idiot, but he thought he'd moved on, moved himself into the friend zone. It was what he'd been trying to do, but somehow he'd failed.

At The Roost, when Emilie had said she was dining alone there'd been something in her eyes that had got him right in the chest, had made him want to be there for her, and when she'd asked him about her portion sizes, all that vulnerability swimming in her eyes, he'd felt that he had to be truthful, because she deserved honesty, friendship, the best of him—

and a break from Buck Island! It was why he'd asked her to spend the afternoon with him.

Being with Emilie had felt so easy. Talking to her had opened him up in a way he hadn't expected. With her, he hadn't been 'the quiet one' at all. For some reason he'd thrown open doors, pulling out things that he hadn't quite known were there, resentment about Lars curdling in his belly, giving his voice that bitter edge. It had been a shock, realising how deep those feelings ran, but he'd felt lighter for airing them. *Emilie* had lightened him, lifted his mood.

After she'd told him about Tom, about how he'd persuaded her to leave a job she loved only to pull the rug from under her in every which way, he'd been determined to lighten her mood too, make her smile again. On the walk back to the distillery he'd dredged up every amusing sailing anecdote he could think of to make her laugh, to see her eyes shining again. And just when he'd thought he was winning she'd started stressing about how she was supposed to be on Buck Island preparing his dinner.

Emilie! So driven, so conscientious, so insecure. He'd found it impossible to watch her churning away, being so damn hard on herself, so he'd taken control, told her that he was taking her out for dinner. That was when everything had started to slide.

At Clara's he hadn't been able to take his eyes off her. Low sun on her face, the little frowns of concentration as she'd tasted things, the million ways her lips could move. She knew all the seasonings, knew which ingredient had been added in which order. He hadn't felt hungry. All he'd wanted to do was watch her. And then he'd realised that Emilie was blowing him off course with her smile and with the sweet light in her eyes. On the boat, he'd taken himself in hand, told himself to stop fantasising about Emilie because they were friends and that was all. *Friends!* By the time he'd been tying up the boat at the jetty, he'd felt sure that he was back on track, then he'd walked her home...

He folded his arms over his head, groaning inside. Walking beside her under the trees, with the splashes of light and the heady scents, his senses had skewed. All he'd wanted to do was kiss her, but she'd run away. Why had he followed?

He squeezed his eyes shut, mining his emotions. Because they'd shared the day, shared pieces of their lives. They'd laughed and cried and, in his case, ranted. He'd had to go after her to make sure that she was all right, because...he

felt something shifting, like a log in the grate…
because she was special. He'd let her in, had
given her a piece of himself that he'd never
given to anyone else, not even Astrid. He'd told
her how he *really* felt about his father, everything spilling out because…because she had no
connection to his family. He'd been able to talk
about Lars without being made to feel disloyal.

Cold filled his belly like a tumour. Astrid
had specialised in construction law because
she'd always been destined to join Larsson
Lüning. She'd always been close to Karl, especially after her mother died, and she'd always wanted to make Karl happy. He'd never
questioned that, had never thought he was
bothered by it, but what if, without realising
it, he'd always kept a corner of himself stuck
down…what if he'd never properly been himself with Astrid because of her connection to
the business…*to Lars?* He felt a pinprick, an
ache gathering around it. If he'd felt like that,
then maybe Astrid had too. Had there always
been a little bit of distance between them…?

He rolled himself up slowly, feeling an acid
ache in his belly. His history seemed to be
shattering like a mirror, splinters everywhere,
shards of the past skewing, throwing up dislocated reflections. He'd have to interrogate
those splinters, fit them back together so he

could see the real picture. He massaged his forehead. More than ever, he needed a friend, someone to talk to. *Emilie?* He'd opened up and let her in, and because of it he'd felt so close to her… But had he lost control, lost himself inside her kiss because *he* was lost, and confused—on the rebound—looking for sweet distraction and comfort?

He blew out a long sigh. If he was on the rebound, looking for physical comfort, if he couldn't be sure of his feelings, then his feelings weren't good enough for Emilie. She'd been through enough heartache with Tom. She didn't need the sorry tailings of his confusion.

He got to his feet and reached for the mainsail. At least things hadn't gone too far… And Emilie *had* called after him, said it was okay, so maybe they *could* put the kiss behind them and still be friends. He felt a stab of guilt. He'd glimpsed her through the kitchen door that morning and had turned on his heel, unable to face her, but now he *needed* to see her, to square everything away. He'd make amends, somehow, but first, he had to stow the sails.

'So…you were out with Mr Larsson yesterday…?'

Emilie felt a knot tightening in her belly. She'd known Melinda would be too curious not to call, but she didn't want to talk about Joel. His kiss was still tingling on her lips, and she was in a tangle about it, unsure of what the fallout was going to be, but whatever it was, she needed to deal with it on her own, not be always clinging to other people, leaning on them.

She took a breath to speak, then noticed the kitchen door. 'Sorry, could you hold on a sec…?' She went to close it. Joel didn't seem to be around, but she didn't want to risk him overhearing. She pressed the phone to her ear again, reaching for a breezy tone. 'Hi… so, yeah, I *was* with Joel, but it's nothing. I just bumped into him in Road Town and he asked me if I wanted to visit the distillery with him…' Not quite the truth, but near enough. 'It sounded like fun, so I went.'

'Uh-huh…'

She held in a smile. Melinda could say so much without saying any actual words. 'We did the tour, then we did the forest trail. Joel wanted to go up to the lookout point, but I was running out of time, so he offered to bring me back. It seemed sensible so I called Erris to cancel—'

'And Erris told *me* that Joel didn't get back to the house until after nine.'

'Ah!' She swallowed hard, trying not to

think bad thoughts about Erris. 'That's because we had dinner at Clara's Kitchen. Joel likes street food and since he was bringing me back, I could hardly say no.'

'Hmm…' Melinda's voice was teetering on the edge of laughter. 'I can see that you were in quite a predicament…'

'Melinda!' In spite of herself, she could feel a giggle vibrating in her belly.

'I'm only teasing.' Melinda was chuckling and then her tone shifted, became gentle. 'I think you had a nice time though, didn't you?'

How could Melinda read her so well? She felt the knot in her belly loosening, memories unspooling, blue-grey eyes burning into hers: *'It's the most beautiful thing I've ever seen…'* Maybe talking about it *would* help. She bit her lips together. 'Yes, I did. I like him, Melinda, a lot. He's a really good guy.'

'I could see that when I was showing him around, not that he said much, but…' there was a little pause '…with some people you can just tell.'

She pictured Tom, felt her heart shrinking. 'Can you though?'

Melinda made a little tutting noise. 'That's just the hurt talking.'

'Probably!' She blew out a sigh. 'I'm not in the best place and Joel's been through some stuff too, *and* he's only here for a couple of weeks so—'

'Stop thinking so hard.' Melinda's voice was like nectar. 'You're in the Caribbean now. Go with the flow, honey. If you like him and he likes you then enjoy it for what it is. God knows you deserve some sweetness after everything you've been through.'

Sweetness? Was Melinda encouraging her to have a fling? She didn't see herself as a fling kind of person, and yet, if Joel hadn't walked away last night, would she have put the brakes on? She closed her eyes, remembering his perfect mouth, the heat inside it, the way he'd tasted on her tongue, that deep, warm smell he had, the hard crush of his body. Heat pooled in her belly. She hadn't been going to say anything about the kiss, but suddenly she needed to let it all out. 'Melinda...' she swallowed hard '...he kissed me.'

A deep rich chuckle filled her ear. 'And how was it?'

She felt warmth flooding into her chest. 'Sublime! It was heart-stopping, toe-curling, mind-blowing. Every cliché you can think of!'

'You're lucky! Some people go their whole lives without ever feeling that with someone.'

Then why didn't she feel lucky? She'd spent the morning in turmoil, wondering how Joel was feeling, wondering where he was and whether they really were still friends, then worrying that she was only doing half the job she was being paid to do, breaching her contract. She stared at the island unit. Well, maybe not today. It was covered with the roast medallions of pork, the corn meal dumplings, the fried plantains and the *callaloo* she'd made. Street food. For Joel.

She bit her lip. 'So you think I should be more laid back about…*things*?'

'I think you should take *things* as they come and enjoy the break because when Mr Larsson… *Joel*…leaves, we're back to a full house. You're gonna be busy!' A little fretting noise suddenly filled the earpiece. *Ben!* Melinda must have been holding him all this time. 'I've got to go. This young man wants a feed.'

She felt a lump filling her throat. 'I can't wait to meet him.'

'And you will, next week! And if you want to invite Joel to the party, go right ahead. He's welcome.'

Would Joel want to go? He liked peace and quiet and if Anton and his troupe were performing it would be nothing short of a carnival! But, if she asked him to go, then maybe it could reseal their friendship, help to smooth over the confusion of the night before. It was something to hope for. 'You're so kind, Melinda, welcoming strangers to your celebration.'

'You're not a stranger! You're my other daughter! And Joel is your friend so you're both welcome, always. Now, you just take care of yourself.' And then she was gone.

'You're my other daughter!'

A glow filled her heart. Talking to Melinda had made her feel better. To think she'd almost kept everything to herself, wanting to be independent, not wanting to be clingy. She turned her phone over and over in her hands. Melinda had never made her feel as though she was clinging and neither had her grandmother, but Tom had—especially towards the end—and at times so had her parents and her sisters.

Funny how the people who were supposed to love her, but who'd never seemed to have, or been prepared to make, enough room in their lives for her, were the ones who'd accused her of being clingy. She sucked in a breath. Maybe the problem wasn't all hers!

She put her phone down and surveyed the spread laid out on the island unit. *So much food!* What had she been thinking? Absently, she knotted her shirt around her waist. The truth was that she hadn't been thinking, not about food anyway. She'd arrived early, hoping to catch Joel so they could talk about things straight away, but he hadn't appeared and there'd been no evidence that he'd had breakfast.

And then she'd started thinking about him—*that kiss*—wondering if they'd be able to get past it, then she'd been worrying about not giving him enough to eat, and all the while, in a sort of trance, she must have started throwing dishes together based on what they'd had at Clara's. Enough to feed an army, but where was he?

Sailing? She went outside and across the terrace, passing the pool, until she was at the parapet. She looked down to the beach, felt her heart skittering. He was there, lying on the catamaran, arms folded over his head. The mainsail and jib were lowered. So, not sailing then, just...what? Avoiding her? She drew in a long, steadying breath. If he was feeling awkward about what had happened the night before, there was no shame in it. She was in the same boat, but they needed to confront it, put real trust in one another, not by playing games on the beach, but by talking.

For a beat she held her breath, measuring the impulse that was stirring in her chest, then she turned, heading back to the house. She felt a connection with Joel, but she wasn't clinging and it didn't have to end in heartache. Heartache only happened if the heart was involved and her heart wasn't. Joel did strange things to her pulse and his kiss was definitely the best thing she had ever tasted, but she could be strong, strong enough to push past all that. She didn't *need* him, but she liked him. She liked his smile, liked the way he made her feel when he looked at her.

'You're in the Caribbean now. Go with the flow.'

She felt a smile edging on to her lips. Whatever it was that had started flowing with Joel was nice. He made her feel special and, maybe, if she hurried, she'd be able to make him feel special too…

'Hey, Joel!'

Emilie! His heart lurched and his teeth crunched as his head struck the metal underside of the rear beam. *'Skit!'*

'Oh, God! I'm sorry…' Her voice was getting closer. 'I didn't mean to startle you. Are you all right?'

He tested his jaw, glad that the hulls on either side of him and the trampoline above him were hiding his face. 'I'm fine.' He rubbed the top of his head hard. 'Just…give me a second, okay?' He snatched a breath, felt shame scorching a hole in his chest. He'd fled from the house first thing because he hadn't been able to face her and now she'd come to him. He felt wrong-footed, awkward, ungallant.

'What are you doing?' There was a bright ring to her voice that sounded slightly forced.

'Stowing the sails. I'm nearly done.' He gritted his teeth and gave the mainsail a final shove before scooting clear of the platform and rocking back to his heels.

She was standing on the leeward side of the hull in loose denim cut offs and a white shirt, knotted at the waist, exposing a tantalising portion of smooth, taut midriff. Her hair was tied up loosely, tendrils blowing against the soft curve of her neck. He felt heat curling in his belly and pulsing in his groin.

She pushed her sunglasses up. 'How's your head?'

He touched the tender spot on his crown, hiding a wince with a smile. 'I'll live. It probably sounded worse than it feels.'

'Actually...' Her face brightened. 'I've got some ice!' She dropped to her knees and started unzipping a large cool bag which he hadn't noticed until that very moment. Her eyes flicked up, holding his. 'I also have lunch, so I hope you're hungry...'

Uncertainty in her eyes, but she'd come anyway. He felt tenderness blooming in his chest.

She was being strong, not letting what had happened come between them, and her strength was bolstering his own, giving him something to lean on. He felt a smile taking over his face as he ploughed towards her on his knees. 'I'm not bothered about the ice, but I *am* hungry!'

Her eyes twinkled. 'Just as well since I've radically upped the portion sizes!' She smiled, handing him a folded-up tablecloth. 'Could you spread that out?'

'Sure!' He toyed with the fabric. She was being breezy, but he could feel the ghost of their kiss shimmering in the air. He needed to exorcise it. The problem was, he didn't know what to say. He unfurled the cloth, anchoring the edges while she plonked down plastic boxes, plates and cutlery. When she shot him a little smile, it suddenly struck him that maybe all he had to do was open himself out like the cloth, see what could be laid down on it. He inhaled a slow breath. 'Emilie, do you want to talk about last night?'

Her hands stilled and then she looked up. 'I do if you do.' Her gaze was soft, filled with gentle curiosity.

He felt his shoulders loosening, his imaginary elevator taking him up a floor. This was already better, feeling that whatever place they were in, they were in it together. He slid a hand to the back of his neck, trying to forget the way she'd tasted, the way she'd wanted him. 'I don't want you thinking that I stopped because of you…because I didn't want to…'

Her tongue touched her lower lip. 'But you did stop.'

'Because I can't…' Splinters and shards glittered inside his head. He swallowed. 'I don't know if I can trust myself any more.'

'Yourself?' She was frowning. 'After what you've been through, I'd have thought that trusting someone else would be the hard part—'

'But that's the thing.' He felt a wave of hopelessness. 'I have a feeling that it's *me*. That there's something wrong with me…something I'm not seeing about myself.'

'Joel…' She was looking at him carefully. 'What happened with your fiancée?'

He tuned in to the sound of the waves. What had happened was simple enough. It was the whole big *before* that he was struggling with now, the *before* that was coming in and out of focus, bending his brain, giving him an acid ache in his stomach.

'Joel…?'

He blinked. Emilie had been so open about Tom and Rachel, but he didn't have a story. There was no ruined business, no cheating partner, well, not exactly. He shrugged. 'Nothing *happened.* Astrid realised that she didn't love me enough to marry me, that's all.' He checked in with his heart, then carried on. 'She thought that she was falling for my brother, Johan.'

'What?' Her eyes were wide, blazing into his. 'That's… It must have torn you apart.'

Like she'd been torn apart. That was what she was thinking. She was joining dots, finding ways to empathise with him because she was all feeling, all heart, but for some reason her kindness was making him feel like a fraud. He scooped up a handful of sand, tightening his fist around it. 'It tore me up for a minute or so and then the tearing stopped!' Saying it out loud was making his neck prickle. 'I told you before, I feel like I'm in limbo. I'm dislocated.' He bit down on his lip. 'I'd thought that maybe it was the shock, but it's been eight weeks now—*eight* weeks—and I'm still waiting to find out where it hurts.'

She was chewing her lip. 'Were you together long?'

Why did that question make everything feel worse? He loosened his fingers, letting sand stream through his fist. 'Since we were teenagers. Astrid was my first girlfriend.' He dusted his hands together, felt his cheeks going warm. 'I'm rather unworldly, I suppose.'

She blinked. 'So am I.' She reached two

beers out of the cool bag and handed him a bottle opener. 'How did you meet her?'

Another question that seemed to be stirring the acid in his stomach. He blew out a breath. 'Astrid's father, Karl, is Lars's business partner, so our families are—' he crossed his fingers '—like this! That said, I only got to know Astrid properly after her mother was killed in a car accident. Karl brought her to the island for the summer. She's an only child. Maybe he thought that being with us would help.'

A shadow flitted across Emilie's eyes. 'You looked after her, didn't you?'

His heart bumped. He'd never looked at it that way. He shrugged. 'I think we just hung out because we both liked sailing.' He opened the beers and they chinked bottles. 'Anyway, that's how it started.' He tasted the beer, then swigged. Emilie's eyes were on him, wanting more. Maybe talking would help. He peeled back a loose edge of the bottle label.

'Astrid's a lawyer, a specialist in construction law. She always intended to work for Larsson Lüning, but she was getting experience elsewhere in the meantime. Sadly, Karl has Parkinson's disease and a few months ago his health deteriorated sharply, so Astrid had to step up and take her place on the Board.

'She was working closely with Johan and I guess...'

Emilie's eyes were glistening. 'Rachel was my best friend; I still can't believe she did what she did, but your brother...? That's beyond bearable.'

He pictured Johan, larger than life, popular with his friends, fiercely loyal to the family and to the business. He shook his head. 'They weren't having an affair, I know that. Johan is too straight, too loyal. It's exactly as Astrid said it was. She was getting to know Johan, feeling things that made her question her feelings for me.' He felt a sharp twist in his gut. 'But even so, to lose the only woman you've ever loved, ostensibly to your brother, and to *not* feel broken...?' His heart was thudding, drumming in his ears. 'It makes you question yourself and everything you thought you knew. It makes you ask yourself—*What have I been doing all this time?*' He pressed the bottle hard against his forehead. 'Turns out I don't know the answer, and if I don't know, then how can I trust myself?'

Emilie ran the tip of her tongue over her lower lip. Joel was zipping up the cool bag, his strong forearms moving deftly, his biceps flexing. It was hard not to stare, hard not to remember the way those arms had felt around her. At least he'd put on a tee shirt before they'd started eating. It would have been impossible to swallow a single bite staring at his tanned muscular chest.

He looked up. 'Street food on the beach! Genius! Thank you.' His eyes flickered with something that made her pulse vibrate. 'And… thank you for listening.'

Listening had been hard, seeing his pain, because she *could* see pain folding him in half, even though he said he was numb. And that pain was making her want to reach out and touch him, take it all away. The sea breeze was playing in his hair, blowing tangled locks into his eyes. She felt her fingers itching with the memory of its softness. *Breathe.* 'You don't have to thank me for listening. You listened to me too, remember…'

He smiled, then pushed the bag aside and moved closer. 'So we're still friends. We're cool after last night?'

Maybe it was the alcohol, or the warmth of his gaze, but suddenly, the sand seemed to be shifting beneath her knees. She wanted to kiss him, taste his lips again. The words he'd spoken were spiralling around in her head. *What have I been doing all this time?* Tom had left four months ago, but he'd stopped reaching for her a long time before that and she'd stopped reaching for him too. How long had she been holding on to nothing? She felt tears scalding her eyes.

'Hey...' Joel's hand covered hers, squeezing gently. 'What's wrong?'

Concern in his eyes, but there was something else too, something that seemed to be flowing out of him and she wanted to pull it around her shoulders, cocoon herself inside it. She rose on to her knees, looking into his eyes. 'Joel, what are *we* doing?'

His hand shifted to her waist, a steadying grip that made her belly flutter. 'What do you mean?'

'I mean...' Her pulse was pounding in her throat, but she couldn't stop now. Something was taking hold of her, heat, longing, muscle memory from the night before. She touched his temples, running her fingers down his jaw, through the soft thatch of his beard.

'Emilie...' His voice was low, ragged around the edges. He was right on the ledge with her and she wanted them to fall, together. She wanted some sweetness. After all the pain they'd been through, was that so wrong?

She swallowed. 'I'm tired of wasting time, Joel.' Something flickered behind his eyes. *Agreement?* It was enough. She leaned in, kissing his upper lip first, tasting, lingering over its soft rub, then she kissed his lower lip, drawing the tender heat of it into her mouth until a groan rumbled from somewhere deep in his throat, then his mouth was taking over, his lips scorching hers, and she was being pulled on to his lap but still, even with his strong hand at her back drawing her in, she couldn't get close enough, couldn't make her heart beat fast enough.

'Emilie...' It was more of a gasp than a word and then he was lifting her, lowering her on to the sand, crashing down beside her. His leg slid over hers and then his hand was under her knee, hitching her leg higher and closer, until she could feel the full hard length of him pressing against her belly. Then his lips were on hers again, but it was a slower kiss now, tender, yearning, every stroke of his tongue fuelling a deep immeasurable longing in her belly.

She slipped her hand under his tee shirt, stroking his smooth warm skin, losing herself in his deepening kiss, and then his hand was roaming too, teasing her breast, sliding over her hip, cupping her rear and it was too much to be feeling, too much. Then his lips moved from her mouth to her neck, scorching a ragged path to her ear. 'What are we doing, Emilie?'

She felt his heart pounding through her skin, saw the heat haze in his eyes, but there was no confusion there, only longing and something else that made it hard to breathe. *Go with the flow.* She buried her fingers into his hair, pulling him in again. 'We're going with the flow, giving our hearts and minds a rest from all the things we can't fix.'

'Going with the flow?' The corner of his mouth lifted, dimpling his cheek. 'I'm not sure that this is—'

'Please, Joel. Don't let's think too hard.' Was she really saying this? 'Let's live in the moment, no strings okay, just us, just this...'

He seemed to hesitate, then he was shifting his leg, rolling sideways.

Her heart caved. She drew her arms over her face, feeling exposed. Stung. What had she been thinking? *No strings!* She wasn't a fling kind of person, or was she? There'd never been a chance to find out because she'd only ever been with Tom. Was going with the flow the same as playing around? Kissing Joel didn't feel like playing around. It felt real, meaningful, but maybe that was her imagination, a reflection of her own neediness. He'd kissed her back, had seemed to want her, but—

'Emilie!'

She sucked in slow breath, lowering her arms.

He was holding out his hand, eyes still blue and hazy. 'Let's go.'

She bit her lip. 'Where?'

He smiled. 'Anywhere that's private and sand-free.'

CHAPTER NINE

EMILIE SMILED FOR the hundredth time and she was glad that Joel couldn't see because it was a silly, giddy, smile with raggedy, wobbly edges. *That* was what two mind-blowing hours in bed with him had done to her. She felt the slow spread of a luxurious tingle. Maybe regret would come when the tingling stopped, but thinking about that was impossible when he was behind her, planting kisses into her hair. She nestled against his chest, lifting her toes to turn on the tap. 'Does this feel decadent to you?'

He shifted a little, then his warm breath was filling her ear. 'Lying in the bath with a beautiful woman…in the middle of the afternoon…in the Caribbean…?' His lips grazed the skin behind her lobe. 'I would say so.'

She twisted so she could see his face, felt her heart skipping. 'Are you happy?'

'Yes…' His eyes were hazy. 'It's a long time since I've felt like this.'

This? She snuggled back against him. She wouldn't ask. Couldn't! Asking him to pin feelings to what they'd just shared would be going against the *no strings* spirit. *No strings!* Her stomach dipped. What *had* she instigated? She wasn't remotely casual about relationships and Joel wasn't a player. He'd called himself unworldly—not that she'd have guessed it from the way he'd made love to her—and yet, on the beach, in the heat of the moment she'd scribbled out a script for them to follow—go with the flow—and he'd followed without too much encouragement. The thing was, not to read anything into that.

She pressed her lips together. Giving in to the attraction they'd been feeling was probably inevitable because they were in the same boat, damaged goods, looking for comfort. She spun the tap with her toes, shutting off the flow. She'd opened a casual door, but sifting through Joel's looks and words, looking for deeper meanings, wasn't going to help her close it again, even if the look in his eyes had stilled her heart.

'If you like him and he likes you, then enjoy it for what it is.'

Melinda's wisdom! What this was, was a fling. That was how she'd sold it to Joel, so she'd have to put a chain around her heart because her heart was going to be her biggest problem. On the beach, when Joel had been talking about Astrid and his brother, she'd felt it flowing out to him in great big waves, but she'd have to curb that instinct. Fantastic sex was one thing, but imagining that it could lead to anything more, hoping that it could, would be like putting her hand in the fire. She'd been burnt badly enough with Tom and she couldn't put herself through that again. She liked Joel, liked the way he made her feel, but this was a band aid, a temporary friendship...*with benefits!*

She closed her eyes, breathing in slowly. This moment was only this: it was the firmness of his body; it was the sweet smell of the oils she'd added to their bath; it was his fingers tracing a line down her arm. Those were the sensations she could believe in, the things she could cling to if she must, but she couldn't ask for more, hadn't thought she wanted more... She pushed the thought away and picked up his hand. 'You're going wrinkly!'

He shifted a little. 'Well, we have been in here for a while.'

She turned round, kissing his chin. 'Maybe we should get out before we dissolve.'

His eyebrows arched. 'I could think of worse ways to go.'

'Dissolving?' She scrunched up her face. 'Ugh!'

He was straightening his legs, forcing her upwards, eyes full of mischief. 'I meant dissolving into you.'

Maybe it was already happening. Her thighs felt as though they were melting into his, melting into the warm fragrant water swirling around them.

His eyes were darkening. 'I think we should give it a try.' His hands were sliding under her behind, easing her closer. She felt the dizzy drag of desire, felt his lips grazing hers. Her breath hitched. Straddling him, skin to skin, in the warm, deep water was stealing her focus, overloading her senses. It was too much… Almost! She smiled for the hundredth and second time, then kissed him back slowly. 'Okay.'

Joel scanned the modest sitting room, feeling the twitch of a smile around his mouth. He hadn't noticed anything about the interior on the way in because they'd tumbled through the door kissing, tugging at buttons and zips, Emilie yanking at his tee shirt. So much for exorcising the ghost of a kiss! Being cool—being friends—had lasted all of five minutes. Having a heart to heart had led to them being literally heart to heart, twice in bed and once in the tub. Maybe it had been inevitable. Playing games on the beach, flirting at the distillery... Last night, Emilie's kiss had lit a fuse. On the beach when she'd kissed him again—such a tender, irresistible kiss—going with the flow had felt like the easiest thing in the world. But now what?

A sudden ache caught him between the temples. Emilie drew him like a magnet. He felt so completely present in her company, but he wasn't whole, wasn't in any kind of place for a relationship. Allowing himself to get attached would be insane, would muddle him up. He was passing through, only here for another couple of weeks, and he needed to solve the puzzle of Astrid, needed to make peace with the past because if he didn't, he'd never find peace in himself.

He crossed to the kitchen sink, filled a glass, then turned, leaning against the counter. When they'd been making love, something in Emilie's eyes had made him feel so alive, so *wanted,* that his lungs had emptied out, but she'd said, 'No strings.' No wonder! She'd been through so much with Tom. Tom was the reason she'd run away from him on the path the night before. She'd said she'd felt scared of kissing *him* because...

He sighed. She hadn't needed to say the rest. He got it. She was bruised by the past and kissing meant letting someone in, letting someone get close. *Usually!* He raked his teeth over his lip. They hadn't discussed rules, but tacitly they'd agreed. They were living in the moment. No strings! He sipped, then set the glass down. He'd never had a fling before. It was all new and a little confusing.

He ran his eyes over the worktop. At the far end there was a fruit bowl stacked with mangoes and bananas, and… He blinked. A Rubik's cube? He went to pick it up, turning it over, looking at the jumbled squares on every face. That was him! Jumbled up, veins still tingling from that mind-blowing session in the bath. Had sex ever felt that good with Astrid?

He closed his eyes. That second summer on the island, he'd spent a lot of time noticing Astrid's body. He might have been too shy to ask any of the girls at school out on a date, but he'd been as horny as any other seventeen-year-old boy. He'd caught Astrid checking him out too. There'd been a lot of 'accidental' hand-brushing when they'd been folding sails or passing a soda back and forth, then they'd started holding hands and kissing in the boat house. There'd been fire, but had they really been burning for each other, or simply burning with the novelty of teenage love? He felt a cloak of heaviness swathing his chest. He'd learned how to please Astrid in bed, but when was the last time she'd actually *looked* pleased? He opened his eyes, staring at the swaying palms and the ribbon of sea framed by the window. When had he stopped seeing Astrid, noticing her…and when had she stopped noticing him?

'Hey!' Emilie was padding across the floor towards him, smiling. She was wearing loose pants and a lightweight sweatshirt, her hair damp around the edges. Her face was still a little flushed. Her eyes darted to his hands. 'Whoa! You've solved it!'

He looked down, surprised. He hadn't even noticed his fingers moving.

'How did you do that so quickly?' Her eyes were wide. 'I can't have been more than two minutes getting dressed.'

He felt a vague uneasiness, like a shadow passing. 'I was a geeky kid. I practised a lot.' He swallowed. 'Is it yours?'

She nodded, taking it from him. 'My grandmother gave it to me years ago. She found it in a charity shop. Talk about *random*, but I'm kind of attached to it! I call her Ruby!' She was twisting it, jumbling it up again. 'I like the mechanics, the way it slides, but I've never been able to solve it!' She handed it back to him, smiling. 'Show me how you do it.'

His heart lurched, then a cold wave ran through him. *'Show them you're the best, Joel! You'll beat them all! Get out there, son, and show them.'*

'Joel! Are you okay?' She was in front of him, a frown settling around her mouth.

He swallowed hard. His pulse was banging. 'Yes…' He forced a smile out. 'Just a flashback.'

'To…?'

He felt the corners of his mouth tightening. 'Lars…'

Emilie seemed to hesitate, then she took a breath. 'Do you want to talk about it?'

He looked at her. Gentleness in her eyes, acceptance. It was nothing of a story, yet the memory had made his heart jolt. Maybe he *should* peel the corner back since talking to her had lightened him before. He shrugged. 'I got a cube when I was seven. I was fascinated by it, loved the process of solving it. I got pretty quick at it.'

'How quick?'

'When I was eight, I was doing it in sixteen seconds or thereabouts.'

She blinked. 'That's amazing!'

He felt his gut twist. 'Lars thought so too.' He swallowed. 'He started taking me to speed-cubing events, entering me...' He swallowed again. 'I went along with it to please him, but I hated it. When you asked me to show you, it came back. The ridiculous pressure!' He felt his neck prickling, a distant anger coming closer, building like a storm cloud. 'I was a quiet kid, shy. I didn't like being looked at, watched, but Lars was always pushing. If you were good at something, you had to push it to the max. He'd never let a little thing just be a little thing!'

Emilie put her hand his arm. 'Maybe he was just proud of you. If you were shy, he might have thought that competing would bring you out of your shell...'

Her touch felt soothing, like balm. He drew in a calming breath. 'Lars *was* proud, but he couldn't see that I was happy just getting faster on my own. *That* wasn't good enough and *competing* wasn't good enough either.' He took a breath. 'It's always been about winning with Lars. I can accept that he's wired that way, but he's never been able to accept that I'm not.'

She was frowning. 'Is that why you didn't want to go into the family business?'

'Because of ancient resentment over speedcubing competitions? No!' *Laughable!* He lifted the cube, inspecting each face, then started twisting. 'I hated those competitions, but I've moved on.' He felt his fingers flying. 'I don't do anything *because* of my father, or to spite him. I didn't join Larsson Lüning because I had my *own* business to grow. I'm my own person; I always have been.' He gave the cube a final twist and held it up, smiling. 'There you go!'

'Blimey!' Emilie's mouth fell open. 'You're a prodigy.'

'Here!' Joel's eyes were twinkling. 'Your very first Painkiller cocktail!'

'Impressive!' She'd seen Painkiller chalked on boards outside the bars in Road Town, but she'd never had the time or the opportunity for sundowners before. She inspected it while Joel was settling himself beside her on the veranda step. It was rum-based, yellow because of the pineapple juice, opaque because of the cream. He'd garnished it with a slice of orange and a sprinkle of nutmeg. She nudged his shoulder. 'The freshly grated nutmeg's a nice touch!'

'I wanted it to be perfect for you.' He kissed her softly. 'You set a high bar.'

The deep look in his eyes swept her back into bed, to the way he'd held her gaze as he'd moved inside her, adjusting his rhythm to every catch of her breath. She felt a blush coming. 'Not with cocktails. I think you're the cocktail *daddy!*' She lifted her glass, then had a thought. 'How do you say cheers in Swedish?'

His chin dipped. '*Skål*, but we don't chink glasses.'

'What do you do?'

A corner of his mouth lifted and his cute dimple appeared. 'There's a whole routine...'

'Go on...'

'Well, first you must make eye contact and maintain it...'

She fastened her eyes on his, felt a giggle bubbling up in her belly.

His fingers tapped the middle of his chest. 'And then you lift your glass to here...'

'Okay.'

'And then you say...' His eyebrows were sliding up.

She tried to copy his accent. '*Skål!*'

He laughed roundly. 'Very good, so, then—'

'You drink?'

'No!' His brow furrowed. 'First you must nod at the person you're toasting with.'

She nodded deeply.

'Perfect!' His eyes were twinkling. 'And then you drink.'

'Hallelujah!' She took a sip and held it, letting the flavours unwind on her tongue. It was soft, sweet, tangy. Intensely alcoholic. She swallowed. 'You might have to make more of these—'

'And, finally…' He was twinkling at her, holding up a finger.

'What! There's more?'

He grinned. 'You have to nod again.'

'With the eye contact?'

'You got it!' He was laughing, eyes full of soft light. 'See. Super easy!'

Super easy! That was how it felt, sipping cocktails with Joel. Smiles and easy laughter, his eyes twinkling, but when he'd been talking about his father, his eyes had looked hollow, wounded. His father was a like cloud hanging over him and she wanted to dig deeper, to help him, soothe him, but those impulses were impulses of the heart and this wasn't meant to be about hearts. This was a fling.

She looked down into her glass, veins skittering, a knot twisting in her belly. She'd opened the door to a throwaway romance, but was she strong enough to keep her heart locked up? She swallowed hard. She thought Tom had ruined her heart, but she could feel Joel, wandering among the debris, looking for a foothold and that wasn't meant to be happening—

'Emilie?' She looked up. He was dangling his glass, elbows parked on his knees, low sun filling his eyes, sharpening his irises into a bright clear blue. So handsome. 'When am I going to be able to visit your café?'

She felt her heart bump, her thoughts tangling. Even if he was actually being serious, there'd be no café to come to unless Tom paid her out and that was unlikely to happen any time soon. She drew an uncomfortable breath. 'I don't know. I only got the idea a couple of days ago...' She forced out a smile. 'It's percolating.'

He jiggled the ice in his glass. 'But it's a good idea. You *must* do it.'

'It's not that easy.'

'Why?'

'Because I don't have the money—' She bit down hard on her tongue. Joel was wealthy. Telling him she was hard up was tantamount to holding out a begging bowl and nothing had been further from her mind. The truth had popped out spontaneously because of the interest in his eyes—his warmth, his friendship, that was all—and now she was mired. She snatched a breath. 'I mean, not at the moment...'

He frowned. 'But if Tom is keeping the bistro and you were equal partners, then he owes you money, right?'

'Yes.' Tears were thickening in her throat.

He was leaning in. 'So—he needs to fork out.'

She swallowed hard. 'It's complicated.'

He took her glass, setting it down with his

own, and then he was taking her hands in his, chafing her fingers gently. 'What's so complicated?'

She blinked. 'Tom can't pay right now because he's moving to a bigger place...' The kindness in his eyes was making her wilt. She felt a tear sliding hotly down her cheek, a wave she couldn't hold back. 'Rachel's pregnant. He's going to be a father.' She raked her teeth over her lower lip. 'It was why he had to come clean about his affair.'

'*Kristus!*' Joel's fingers tightened around hers.

'When he told me, I knew I was losing everything—everything I'd worked for and more than ten years of my life—but what hurts the most is that Tom's going to have a family, just like that, and I'm back to square one.' Her throat closed and suddenly there was no point trying to hold Joel's gaze, no point trying to stop her tears.

'*Hjärtat!*' He breathed the word and then she was being folded into his arms, warm and tight and close and it felt so nice, as though she was being protected. Cherished. She didn't want to move, so she stayed there, talking into his damp tee shirt, feeling steadier with every breath.

'I don't know when Tom and I stopped talking about anything other than the restaurant. Towards the end we didn't even talk about that because it always ended in an argument. We never talked about marriage, or children. It was all work—probably my fault because, for some reason, I'm driven in that way—but it was in the back of my mind, you know. A baby…' She felt tears clawing at her throat again, sucked in a lungful of Joel's deep, comforting, smell. 'It was something for the future. And now that future's gone.'

He shifted back, easing her away from his chest, his eyes gentle. 'You're right, that one has, but the future's still there. It's different, that's all.' A smile touched his lips. 'You never know, maybe it will be a better one.' His eyes held hers for a long second, then he was picking up their glasses. 'I think we need more Painkiller!'

She took a big breath and wiped her face. She hadn't wanted to talk about Tom and Rachel and the baby, but Joel had led her to it so gently, and he'd comforted her. In his arms, nothing had felt so bad. She took another breath, feeling opened out. It was a nice feeling, like being out in a summer rain.

'The future's still there…'

She got to her feet and stepped on to the veranda, leaning forward over the rail. Joel was

right. The future was still there and it was hers
for the taking. It was time to start fighting for
it, time to pursue Tom for the money because
otherwise she'd be dangling, waiting around for
ever, and she was tired of waiting. She checked
herself, felt a sudden ripple of lightness. She
wasn't harbouring any spite for Tom. She just
wanted her money and then she'd be free.

Joel's footstep scuffed behind her. 'Here!
Another dose should do the trick.'

She smiled. 'Shall we do the whole *skål* routine again?'

He leaned over the rail beside her. 'God, no!
Just drink it!'

She sipped, breathing in the soft, fragrant
air. The sea was a low gush. A bird chivvied
its way through the nearby hibiscus bush and
another bird broke cover, taking flight with
a stuttering, indignant cry. Everything felt
mellow, or maybe it was the second cocktail loosening her joints, smoothing out her
creases. Joel was staring into the distance, a
faraway look in his eyes. The breeze took his
hair, blowing it across his eyes, but he didn't
seem to notice. She sighed. She'd feel easier
about the whole fling idea if just looking at
him didn't fill her up to the brim.

He shifted suddenly, fixing serious eyes on
hers. 'Can I ask you a question?'

She nodded.

'If there hadn't been a baby…if Tom had told you he was having an affair, would you have fought for him?'

Her mind blanked. It was a question she hadn't asked herself, a question that seemed too big to answer. She drank the last of her cocktail and parked the glass by her feet. 'I don't know… I'd have to think about it.'

He sighed. 'You were in a no-win situation, but I wasn't.' He pushed his hair away from his eyes. 'I could have fought for Astrid and I didn't.'

She pressed her lips together. He might not have fought for Astrid at the time, but he wasn't letting go either. 'Maybe you felt too hurt. Betrayed! I mean, even if Astrid wasn't actually having an affair, there must have been a moment when you felt turned over, too beaten to fight…' She sighed. 'Or maybe you could just see that there was no point.'

A shadow lengthened behind his eyes. 'Maybe I was indifferent.' He swallowed. 'Scary seeing as I was about to get married.'

It was hard seeing him turning on himself like this. She reached for his hand. 'I suppose the thing to hold on to is you *were* sure once… I mean, you *did* propose.'

'I was twenty-three.'

She bit her lips together. Cynicism on his voice. He was on a downward spiral, and what could she possibly say that wouldn't make him feel worse? To be engaged so young. To be engaged for so long... Why weren't they married already? She wanted to know, but sharing more confidences would only make her feel closer to him and the writing was on the wall. He'd said he felt numb about Astrid, but he was churning away over her all the same. Astrid was on his mind, probably still in his heart too. For her own sake she had to put her heart back on its leash.

He shifted on his feet. 'Emilie, I'm going to go.'

She nodded. He clearly needed some space, and she did too. *No ties!* She stepped in, went up on her toes and kissed him softly. 'I'll see you tomorrow then.'

For a split second, his eyes flickered, maybe with hesitation, and then he smiled. 'Yes. Maybe I could take you sailing...'

CHAPTER TEN

One week later...

JOEL DRAGGED THE catamaran up the beach, then crashed on to the sand, pulling in long, deep breaths. His heart was pounding. He'd just pitchpoled spectacularly, turtling the boat, winding himself.

He inhaled slowly, filling his lungs, feeling his pulse steadying. Sailing while distracted was never a good idea! He should have been watching the swell, throwing his weight aft in time to stop the starboard hull nosing under, but instead he'd been thinking about Emilie, about the first time he'd taken her sailing.

He felt a smile coming. That giddy excitement on her face as the hull had risen high into the air. She'd been laughing and shrieking as he'd tooled the boat across the water, playing the mainsheet, flying the hull. *Flying!* That had been his heart too. Seeing her so crazy-happy had filled him to the brim.

He unzipped his life vest, giving his lungs some space. He'd taken Emilie sailing three times and snorkelling, which she'd never done before. They'd swum with turtles and they'd found a small, secluded stretch of reef teaming with bright, darting fish in rainbow colours, but the best sight of all had been Emilie pushing up her mask, face aglow, her smile like heaven. It had been an amazing week, just living in the moment, feeling free...

There'd been so many great moments, like riding rickety bicycles along paths of winding red packed sand to a lagoon bar where the locals raced hermit crabs for low stakes. In the evenings, she'd insisted on cooking because she'd said she would die of guilt otherwise. That was Emilie, so conscientious!

He'd insisted on taking her out one night, though, to an elegant restaurant in Via Garda. They'd drunk Painkiller cocktails at a beachside table under the stars. She'd made him laugh when she'd whispered to him that the cocktails weren't nearly as good as his.

He dug his hands into the sand, closing his eyes. In bed with Emilie, it felt like something was taking him over, a feeling too pure, too big to hold on to. Maybe it was sexual chemistry, plain and simple, but it scared him because it seemed to have strings dangling from it, and Emilie had said 'no strings'.

He sighed. She might have said it, but so often over the past week it had felt as if the lines were blurring. So often he'd felt the light in her eyes reaching right into his heart, had felt the light in his own beaming right back. *Confusing!* It was why he'd never spent a whole night with her, even though he'd wanted to. It was why he was still going off on his own now and again, although it wasn't the only reason.

He got up, shrugging off the vest and throwing it on to the trampoline. Astrid was still the itch he couldn't seem to scratch, the puzzle he needed to solve, and today, his belly wouldn't stop churning. Emilie had been busy with the finishing touches for the cake she was making for Melinda and Erris's beach party anyway, so he'd split. As long as he was back in time to carry the boxes and drive the boat to Boulder Cay, she'd be cool. *No strings!*

He fished his tee shirt out of his daysack and put it on, scanning the beach. Salt Island was barely inhabited. There were only a handful of buildings idling under a stand of palm trees near the jetty, but running into people was the last thing he wanted to do. That would mean talking and he didn't want to talk. He needed to think. He turned, walking in the other direction, taking a sandy path which wound upwards to the top of a small hill. It was a steep climb and the sun was hot. He felt sweat breaking out around his hairline, a trickle sliding down the side of his temple.

'The thing to hold on to is you were sure once... I mean, you did propose.'

Ever since she'd spoken them, Emilie's words had been clinging to the edges of his consciousness. For some reason he couldn't shake them off. He *had* proposed to Astrid, so he *must* have been sure once, must have been sure for all these years because they'd set the date for the wedding, hadn't they? So why wasn't he broken and bleeding? Why hadn't he fought for Astrid?

'You did propose.'

He strode on, sweating into his tee shirt, picturing his screensaver, the selfie they'd taken... Warm pleased smiles, sparkling eyes, Astrid holding out her ring finger, showing off the ring that had been his grandmother's, the ring that Lars had given him. He stopped, pulse pounding in his throat, a familiar acid ache starting in his belly. Splintered shards were moving together... Their apartment. A party. Their official engagement. Astrid closing the door on the last guest. Collapsing against him.

'At least this'll get Karl and Lars off our backs for a while...'

He felt the ache deepening, expanding, moving upwards into his chest. Karl and Lars. *Pressure!* Had Astrid felt pressured into accepting his proposal? Had she been trying to make Karl happy? Had Karl leaned on her the way that Lars had... Black dots peppered his vision. He fell to his knees, heart hammering like it was pushing his blood backwards. Shards and splinters were flying at him like knives: Lars popping open the ring box.

'You should make it official, son! Propose to Astrid at her twenty-first birthday party. It would mean a lot to Karl right now!'

His temples pounded. Dryness filled his mouth. *Pressure.* Legs trembling. *Pressure.* Like speed-cubing. Hands trembling around the cube. The stopwatch. The fear. *Pressure!*

He rocked forward, gulping air. He'd squared up to Lars. He'd told him he'd propose in his own good time. But he'd taken the ring. *Taken the ring!* Proposed. *Proposed!* Just as Lars had wanted. *Just as Lars had wanted!*

Pain howled in his chest. All this time, he'd thought he was his own person, blazing his own trail, but it wasn't true. He'd done as Lars had asked, some fragment of his eight-year-old self still craving approval, and maybe, deep down, he'd been despising himself for it all this time. It was so clear now. Resentment for Lars had been the wind beneath his wings. He'd built Larlock from the ground up to show Lars that he didn't need *him* or Larsson Lüning and he'd put everything into it. *Everything!* Maybe that was why he'd always kept the Lars corner stuck down, because it was too painful, too hateful to peel back. He sucked in a ragged breath. And what about Astrid? Had she only agreed to marry him for Karl's sake, trying to make him happy because he'd lost a wife and was losing a battle with his health?

No! He sat back on his heels, steadying himself. He couldn't believe that, any more than he could believe that he'd only asked Astrid to marry him because Lars had prodded him with a ring.

'The thing to hold on to is you were sure once…'

He closed his eyes. The waves rolling on to the beach below were a steady gush, rhythmic, soothing. He breathed in deeply, saw cherished shards spangling behind his lids… Astrid in her green beanie. Blue eyes, clear as water. Shy smiles. Bright laughter. Pale hands full of lingonberries. Painting the walls in their first apartment. Walking through the snow in Royal Djurgården…

He felt his chest shaking, something breaking apart inside. Astrid had been his friend, his first love, his rock, and he'd loved her. A sob filled his throat. He *had* loved her, he had, so, so much…but Larlock had taken him over and Astrid's law career had taken a hold of her, and somehow the years had spun by, happiness turning slowly into a sort of bland comfort. They'd stopped sailing together, their love life had dwindled, but they'd gone on, treading water, coasting on the foundations they'd built in earlier times, all the while drifting further and further apart. They'd stopped feeding the fire, stopped loving each other in the right way and their flames had all burned out, but still, they'd carried on.

Had they been afraid to look at what they'd become because of their families' expectations? *'Don't hurt Karl's daughter…'* Had *he* unwittingly been bending under the weight of Lars's unspoken warning for all these years? *Kristus!* They'd even set a date for the wedding. He rolled each shoulder forward in turn, wiping his face on the sleeves of his tee shirt. Maybe Johan had actually saved them! As for Lars—his belly flinched—living under the cloud of his father was killing him and holding on to all that resentment was pointless. Exhausting. He'd have to find a way to let it go.

'Is that why you didn't want to go into the family business?'

Emilie's intuition had been spot on! She wasn't only good with evidence! He breathed in deeply and out again, letting go, wilting. He slid a hand to the back of his neck, digging his fingers into the tightness there. A brown pelican was flying over the sea below, stoop-shouldered, scoop-beaked. He felt his lips twitching. Emilie had been elbow-deep in icing when he'd left, indulging her love of sugar craft, she'd said. She'd made two sugar pelicans and a whole raft of other small creatures and colourful figures. The cake was large and complicated. When it was finished it was going to be less of a cake, more a work of art.

Warmth filled his chest. She was such a perfectionist! She'd blamed herself for letting work come between her and Tom. She'd blamed herself for not talking to him about wanting a family, but Tom could have brought it up! There were two of them in that relationship. She needed to stop blaming herself for everything!

He checked his watch and got to his feet. The quiet café was a good idea, bound to be a success if she could get it off the ground. Emilie had told him that she'd emailed Tom about the money. That was a start! *Tom!* Would he come through? He felt a twinge in his chest. Why was a small part of him hoping that Tom wouldn't? He started down the path, feet sliding in the soft sand. When Emilie had told him about the money situation, he'd wanted to offer her what she needed, but he'd held back. She'd have only felt awkward, or embarrassed, and she'd been upset enough already, crying over the baby. But if Tom paid her out, she wouldn't need his help. She wouldn't need him at all.

The twinge in his chest was spreading into his gut. He stopped to catch his breath, swallowing hard. When Emilie had been crying in his arms, he'd felt an overwhelming desire to protect her, to never let anything hurt her like that again. *Strings!* He walked on. She'd needed him then and he wanted her to keep needing him. He stopped again. The twinge was fading, a strange, wonderful warmth flooding in, a glow that seemed to be getting brighter. He ran his tongue along his lip, trying to fathom it, and then it settled gently in his chest, pulsing a steady warmth.

He faltered, gathering the threads of his feelings together, then his breath stopped. *I love her.* He blinked. *He* wanted to be her everything…the one she ran to…the one who could make everything right… He felt a smile ghosting around his mouth. He was tangled in Emilie's strings, but it felt like freedom, felt like flying the hull with the wind in his hair. Somehow, while he'd been giving his heart and mind a rest, his heart seemed to have made up his mind for him. He was in love—*in love*—and that changed everything.

Emilie tucked the last two sugar pelicans into the crumpled tissue paper, then looked down into the box, staring. The flying fish and the turtles, the hummingbirds and the pair of parakeets seemed nice and secure. She sighed, then clicked the lid shut and put the small plastic box with the bigger boxes which contained the sugar palm trees, the baby and crib, and the Moko Jumbie figures. The cake itself was boxed and in the fridge. Now, all they had to do was get everything to Boulder Cay in one piece. Joel had told her not to worry; he'd said he'd take it easy in the power boat, so nothing would get damaged in transit.

Joel! A warm sad ache filled her chest. He'd taken himself off sailing again, a familiar chink of distance in his eyes. She swallowed hard. He'd gone off on his own a few times. He was obviously still trying to piece together his feelings about Astrid, but she didn't ask him about it. She wanted to—so much—wanted to listen, to help, to fix him, but she'd set the rules. *No strings!* That meant not getting close, not getting involved. She felt tears thickening in her throat. *Too late!*

She took off her chef's jacket, folding it slowly. If Grandma hadn't called that morning, she'd still have been blissfully ignorant about her feelings; she'd have still been looking forward to baby Ben's party instead of dreading it.

Misery pooled in her belly. *Grandma!* She'd only been trying to help...

'You know you were telling me about your wonderful idea for a quiet café? Well, yesterday I had a dental appointment in Salton and, as I was going along the High Street, I noticed a tearoom for sale. It's all shut up, but I looked through the window. It's lovely inside. It could be the perfect thing. It's on with Cox's Estate Agents so you should have a look online, see what you think...'

Her heart should have leapt! A café close to Grandma's village was exactly what she had been hoping for, but instead her heart had withered. In that instant she'd realised that a café in Salton, or anywhere, wasn't what she wanted any more. She wanted Joel. She wanted a future filled with twinkling blue-grey eyes, and sailing, and babies...

She stuffed the jacket into her tote and

started walking. The tears she'd been holding on to all morning were stinging her eyes, making her throat burn.

I love Joel. She went down the steps, swallowing hard. *I love him.*

She clenched her jaw, pushing hard, trying to push it all back inside. How had it happened? She'd set the rules. She'd been so careful, telling herself that she was cool with him not spending the night, cool with him going off on his own. She'd told herself that maybe he was even trying to underline to her that they were having a fling and nothing more. But somehow, in spite of being cool, her heart had latched on. Behind her back it had wrapped itself around him, all warm, because he was sweet and kind, and wonderful. *Special!*

She started along the forest path, hugging her tote. The past week had been better than any week she could remember. Joel had made her feel as if *she* were the one on holiday… He'd taken her sailing. Flying the hull! Such a glorious feeling, being up in the air, skimming through the water with the spray and the wind in her face, her ears full of the breeze and all the alien clinking and flapping and gushing of the boat, and Joel…pulling at the ropes— *sheeting in*—biceps bulging, the splashing spray making his firm, tanned body glisten.

He'd taken her snorkelling too, had shown her a mesmerising underwater world of colour and movement and shimmering light. It had taken her breath away almost as much as the light in his eyes. He'd lined up so much: a hike through the national park, a lagoon swim. They'd drunk cocktails on the deck of a restaurant as the sun went down, ridden dodgy bicycles—which had made them cry with laughter—and in bed, he'd made her feel so good, so wanted, so cherished that it had almost felt...

She hugged her bag tighter, aching inside. Maybe her heart wasn't to blame. So many times over the last week it had felt as if Joel was more than just a friend with benefits. In his arms, telling him about Tom and Rachel's baby, she'd felt so safe, so protected, as if nothing bad could ever happen to her again. That thing he'd said about a different future, a better one... It had given her a boost. She'd been thinking about the café then, had fired off an email to Tom that night, but after that, she must have dropped the ball, started dreaming impossible dreams.

She looked up, blinking at the light glittering through the canopy. Impossible dreams seemed to be her speciality. Dreams of a life with Tom...brown-eyed and smiling in the college kitchen, his dark mop drawn into a ponytail, pale hands rocking the knife…short-haired at Le Perroquet, handsome and bus-tling in his chef's whites…and at Blythe's in his black tee shirt with the Blythe's logo… She felt a sharp ache behind her eyes. She'd worked hard on the logo because branding was important. It set the vibe. White copperplate gothic font against black, Blythe's—*his* sur-name—which she hadn't minded because she'd thought that she'd be Emilie Blythe one day. Her belly knotted tight. Tom was the one who had wanted to leave Le Perroquet. Profession-ally, he'd hit a ceiling. She'd been above him. She'd been happy, doing well, but he'd always had her back and working there without him had seemed impossible, so she'd handed in her notice. She'd given up everything for him and, when the wheels were coming off, she'd hung on, trying to fix things, clinging to old dreams, clinging to Tom, clinging to the food she knew. *Fool!*

A week ago Joel had asked her if she'd have fought for Tom if there hadn't been a baby. How hadn't she known the answer when it was so obvious? She walked up the cottage path and kicked off her sandals against the veranda steps. It was a pitiful—yes! But it wouldn't have been fighting. It would have been cling-ing because clinging was what she did best.

She sank down on to the swing. Would she *never* learn to stop tangling herself up in stupid dreams? This thing with Joel was supposed to have been a little thing, but she'd let it get bigger, allowed herself to imagine that the fond light in his eyes could be… *Fool again!* She felt tears burning in her throat, scalding her lids. Joel had signed up for a fling. Nothing more. The writing was on the wall. He was still beset with Astrid, still taking himself off with distance in his eyes, and he was leaving in a week. *Leaving!*

Pain blocked her lungs. It was over. For a beat there was no air to breathe and then wetness filled her eyes, spilling down her face. If she didn't put the brakes on now, then her heart would shatter when he left. It would be a fierce wrench, but she had no choice. She *had* to step away from Joel, protect herself as best she could. She locked her arms across her belly, holding back a spreading nausea. Going with the flow had been a bad idea. *Bad!* She wasn't a fling kind of person. She was a person who got attached, a person who always got hurt. She swallowed hard. What would Joel make of her cooling things off? Hurting him was the last thing she wanted to do, but telling him she was in love with him was impossible. He'd think she was like Lars, not letting a little thing just be a little thing.

She wiped her face, dragging in air, tasting the salt on her lips. Joel would be okay. He had plenty of other stuff to think about. *Astrid!* She swallowed hard, gulping in more shaky breaths. It would be all right. *She* would be all right. She licked her lips. It wasn't too late to put herself back on track, to find happiness in her own skin, on her own terms, standing on her own two feet. No more fantasies! No more impossible dreams.

She got to her feet. Her dream had been Café Hygge before everything had skewed in a Joel-wise direction. It was still a future she *could* believe in and the place in Salton might well be perfect. She sucked in a big breath, felt her pulse steadying. There was time to look online before she got changed for the party, time to check if Tom had deigned to reply to her email.

CHAPTER ELEVEN

ERRIS HELD THE DOOR. 'Will this do?'

Emilie scanned the space. It was a store-room, a bit pokey, stacked with bright plastic crates full of empty beer bottles but there was a smallish table against the back wall which looked clean and just big enough for a spot of covert cake assembly. 'It's perfect, better than I'd expected.' She smiled. 'I hadn't realised there was going to be a beach bar.'

Erris leaned from side to side, hitching up his shorts. 'We've got our own food, but we hired the bar and the DJ. The private beach comes with it!' He grinned. 'Melinda knows how to throw a party!' His eyes darted to the boxes she was holding. 'And it looks like you know how to make a cake!'

'*This* is the cake!' Joel was coming in with the big box, pretending to stagger. 'What Emilie's got are the decorations.'

Erris's mouth fell open. 'Oh, my!'

Joel grinned, eyes darting to hers. 'It's going on the table, right?'

She nodded, watching him fake-stumbling towards the table. It was impossible not to smile. Why did he have to be being even more charming than usual just when she needed to distance herself? And why did he have to be looking so handsome? His pale khaki shirt made his eyes seem brighter and bluer and he'd shaved his beard closer. He smelt good. Clean. Sexy. She wanted to fold herself into him, breathe him in, but that was off the table now. She steadied the boxes she was holding. Ever since he'd got back from his solitary sail, Joel had been warm and attentive, sweet and affectionate. It was making everything harder, making her heart ache. She'd kept having to dodge his arms, pretending that she was pre-occupied with the cake, anxious about how it would fare in the heat and about her decorations breaking or getting knocked, which had only made him even more attentive, more care-ful. As they'd gone down the steps to the jetty, he'd kept looking back, checking that she was okay with her boxes, such a sweet, protective kind of light in his eyes that she hadn't been able to hold his gaze.

'Erris…?'

Her heart bounced. 'Go!' She parked her

boxes lopsidedly on a beer crate, then steered Erris towards the door. 'Melinda can't know we're here! Go!'

Erris tapped his nose, grinning, then moseyed out into the narrow passage.

She shut the door behind him, pausing for a beat. The prospect of being alone with Joel in such a small space was making her belly quiver. She took a breath and turned around.

He was standing by the table, a new looseness around his shoulders. He seemed relaxed, happy, as if he didn't have a care in the world. He smiled. 'What can I do to help?'

She swallowed. If only she didn't need any help, then she wouldn't have had to be cloistered in this little room with him, but the table was too small to take the cake and all the other boxes so she'd need him to help juggle things. At least assembling it all would keep her legitimately bent to the task, too busy to catch his eye. She crossed to the table and peeled the lid off the cake box. 'Well, first we need to get the cake out. It's on a base and there's a cloth underneath, so we just have to grab the ends of the cloth and lift.'

'Okay.' One corner of his mouth lifted and then he moved behind her, his hands sliding around her waist. His lips grazed her ear. 'I really, really want to kiss you…'

She closed her eyes, fighting an ache of desire, trying to ignore the warm weight of his hands and his clean irresistible scent. She wanted to turn around, slide her hands into his hair, feel his warm perfect lips moulding to hers, but she couldn't. Her heart buckled. It was over, but telling him now, especially when he seemed so happy, would only make things sticky. There was a whole afternoon ahead of them. A whole afternoon to get through. She took a careful breath, then twisted her head to look at him. 'Joel, Melinda's here! We've got to get this done before someone barges in and spoils the surprise.'

He caught her face with his hand, stroking her cheekbone slowly. His gaze was so heart-breakingly tender that it was hard to hold it. And then he leaned in and his lips brushed hers. 'Later, then...'

She nodded, biting back tears.

He moved back to the table, pulling at one of the loose fabric edges with interest. 'The cloth's a neat trick.'

She pulled the cloth out on her side of the box, steadying herself. This was so much harder than she'd thought it was going to be and the way he was looking at her was making it even harder. She took a breath. 'I have a friend who makes wedding cakes! She passed on a few tips.' She gripped the cloth. 'So, we'll lift on three, okay?'

'Yes, chef!'

She couldn't not smile. It felt like a relief, like a moment of normality. She looked up. 'Okay! One...two...three...'

The cake went up and landed perfectly.

As the cloth fell away, Joel's eyes popped. 'Wow! This is amazing! The way you've got the texture of the sea...and the waves...and the sand... Even without the extras it's a work of art!' His eyes caught hers. 'You're a genius!'

'It's a simple rectangle...'

His eyebrows arched. 'No, it isn't and you know it!'

She pressed her lips together. He was right. There was nothing simple about the cake. For one thing, it was vast, enough to feed sixty guests. She'd added height at the beach end, modelling texture in the sand with toasted coconut, and she'd sculpted waves in the sea, as well as adding a ombre effect—turquoise through to deep blue—which she'd continued over the edges and down the sides. Simple wasn't part of her culinary vocabulary. She was always pushing herself, going for the wow factor...except for the food she'd made over the past week. She'd toned things down, making Joel the simpler foods he enjoyed...grilled fish, stews, salads and bread rolls…and it had felt just as rewarding as making the compli-cated stuff. Maybe it was because every time, he'd looked at her as if she'd been giving him the world.

She blinked. Voices were filtering in from the beach, growing louder. Guests were arriv-ing and she needed to get the cake assembled. She went for the boxes she'd left on the crate and put the biggest one into Joel's hands. She peeled off the lid. 'It's going to be a bit dull for you now.'

He smiled. 'Things are never dull with you.'

Despair pooled in her belly. If only he would stop being quite so adoring. It was making everything hurt more. She pinned on a smile. 'There's a first time for everything.'

'Yes, chef!'

His smile was too much. The sooner she was finished and could go out and mingle with the crowd the better. She needed to put some dis-tance between them, otherwise her heart was going to break.

'You shouldn't have gone to all that trouble, honey…' Melinda was drawing her along the beach away from the throng, one warm, plump arm hooked through hers, consterna-tion warring with affection in her deep brown eyes. 'I mean, it's a beautiful cake, Emilie—exquisite—but so much work!' She was shaking her head, making little clicking noises with her tongue. 'And there was me thinking you were having a break, enjoying some downtime.'

She squeezed Melinda's arm. 'I enjoyed doing it.' It had been worth all the effort to see Kesney and Will's delight, and so lovely to see Melinda and Erris beaming, the guests smiling. Even baby Ben's eyes had popped wide when Kesney had held him close to the cake, probably because of the bright colours. 'Besides, you've been so kind inviting me and Joel along that I couldn't *not* bring something.'

'Bringing yourselves would have been more than enough.' Melinda's voice became firm. '*More* than enough.' She stopped walking, pulling her arm free, her gaze suddenly serious. 'You know, Emilie, you need to believe that you're enough, by yourself. You don't always need a passport.'

She felt something small working loose in her chest, something that made her want to cry. She swallowed. 'I know that…of course I do. It's just that…this is such a special occasion. I mean, Ben's your *first* grandchild! I wanted to make something special, that's all.'

'I know that's what you thought you were doing, but I'm just saying…' Melinda's eyes held hers, and then her face changed, softening. 'Joel thinks you're enough.'

'Oh!' Her heart dipped. 'No. I don't think…' She drew her hair over her shoulder, smoothing it down for something to do.

'It's plain to see.' Melinda smiled. 'You only have to look in his eyes.'

Looking into Joel's eyes, losing herself in all that light was the one thing she couldn't do. Not any more. She pressed her lips together. 'We're just friends.'

'Does *he* know that?' Melinda's eyes narrowed. 'I mean, the last time we spoke you were in a fair old swoon about his kiss—'

'I know.' She looked away, neck prickling. That first kiss seemed light years away. So much had happened since then—too much— and now her heart was paying the price. She swallowed hard, meeting Melinda's gaze. 'There's no future in it.'

'How do you know that?'

She licked her lips. 'Because he was jilted at the altar—effectively—and he's all over the place about that.' A choking sadness swelled in her throat. 'He's not ready for a relationship and I'm not either. He's lovely—really lovely— and if circumstances were different…but we're both on the rebound.' She swallowed hard. 'I need to be sensible now, cool things off because he's leaving soon and...'

My heart is breaking already.

Melinda's lips pursed. 'Well, if that's the way you feel, you should tell him.'

'I will...' She bit her lip. 'Not now, but... soon.'

Melinda shook her head a little, sighing, and then she looked over towards the raised deck of the bright green, clapboard beach bar. 'Look! Anton's about to start!'

She followed Melinda's gaze. Sure enough, Anton and his stilt dancers were launching themselves upwards, walking jerkily in the soft sand, their long, red satin trousers rippling, their white satin shirts and red waistcoats glowing in the sinking sun. There were eight dancers, three young women, five young men, all laughing as they helped each other with last-minute costume adjustments. The sound system barked and blared, then started blasting out a lively Soca beat.

Melinda made to walk back. 'Are you coming?'

She nodded. 'I'll be along in a moment.'

Melinda squeezed her arm. 'Honey, stop thinking so hard. Things usually have a way of working themselves out.'

She forced out a thin smile. 'I know. Go with the flow, right!'

She felt her smile fading as Melinda picked her way back along the beach. It was all very well Melinda telling her not to think, but not thinking—going with the flow—was what had got her into this fling situation in the first place, and just believing that things always worked out in the end didn't mean they would.

Tom was proof of that, although, miracle of miracles, he had emailed back. Rachel's parents were stepping up. They were going to buy her out of Blythe's, so she'd be solvent by the time she got back to England. It was what she'd wanted. It meant she could start thinking about the future… Café Hygge. If only she could feel more enthusiastic about it. She swallowed hard, biting her lips. The place in Salton had looked promising. It was definitely something to think about…

Joel! She drew a long breath, looking across the beach, past the ornate braziers fashioned from ancient marker buoys, past the dancers who were lining up to start, to the deck of the bar. He was talking to someone, a beer bottle in one hand, his other hand pressed to the back of his neck. The hand-to-neck thing was what he did when he was unsure of himself. Somehow, she knew that about him, just as she knew every trick of his mouth, and all the shades of light in his eyes.

Guilt ached through her veins. Joel wasn't a party person, but he'd come to be with her and she'd left him to his own devices all afternoon, and now his hand was clamped to his neck because he wasn't at ease. Tears prickled behind her eyes. It wasn't fair, *she* wasn't being fair. Dodging his arms, avoiding him all afternoon was cruel and, whatever she was, she wasn't that. She couldn't put it off another minute. She needed to tell him it was over.

Joel leaned his forearms on the rail, dangling his beer bottle. He was glad the show was in full swing. It meant no more making conversation with yet another person he would never meet again. He sighed. On the beach, Anton was bending backwards at a near impossible ninety degrees, wheeling his arms around, pulling a theatrical *I might fall* face. His agility was incredible. That limbo move would have been difficult enough on the ground, never mind doing it on six-foot-high stilts!

One after the other, the dancers were leaning back too, spinning their arms, then they all hopped upright together and sidestepped across the hard-packed sand before pulling one leg behind themselves so that their stilts were horizontal. After that, the moves kept coming…crouching, stooping, undulating, stilt legs crossing and spinning, sawing diagonally through the air, one dancer even bringing one leg up into a vertical split. It was amazing.

Earlier, Anton had told him how much he loved walking up high, the feeling that in the air anything was possible, and Joel could see it in him, the hard, bright energy pulsing through his body as he danced, all the happiness shining out of his face.

He shifted his gaze, staring at the beer bottle in his hands. Bright, energetic and happy was how he'd been feeling earlier that day, but not now. Now, there was a deep uncomfortable ache spreading through his chest. For some reason Emilie was avoiding him and it hurt. He'd helped her with the cake, carried it out into the bar, but since then it was as if she'd forgotten that he was there. Melinda and Erris had been great, welcoming him warmly, but he wasn't a great socialiser. Not like Emilie. She'd flitted from group to group, chatting easily with Melinda and Erris's family and friends, cradling the baby with such a sweet look on her face, but she'd barely looked at him all afternoon.

He sipped his beer. Maybe he was just being too sensitive about it because he was in love, because he *knew* for certain he was. He'd come to the party to be with Emilie, but she would have come with or without him. Just because he'd tangled himself up in all the strings didn't mean she had, or would. And yet…so many times over the last week he'd seen something behind her eyes that had made his heart beat a little faster, that had seemed to lift him into the light. It was hard to believe that she didn't feel something.

He sighed. That morning when he'd left to go sailing, she'd seemed fine, maybe a little preoccupied with the cake, but that was fair enough. She'd put a lot of work into it and worrying about it melting, collapsing or about the decorations getting broken was understandable. He'd been cool with all that, but he'd hoped that once everyone had seen the cake, she'd have lightened up, turned back into her old self again, even her old 'no strings' self… His heart twisted sharply, making his breath catch. Even in the fling zone, Emilie had been warmer, sweeter, more attentive than she'd been all afternoon. The deep ache in his chest deepened. There had to be something really wrong.

A tide of clapping and cheering broke into his thoughts and he looked up. The dancing was finished. Anton and his troupe were giant-striding towards the bar, slowing through the soft sand, and then they were parking themselves on the red rail, unstrapping their wooden stilts, faces sheened with perspiration.

He straightened, parking his bottle on a nearby table. The bar was colourful: red rails around the deck, green clapboard walls, blue tables with green chairs pulled up, table lanterns in pinks and yellows, and purples, the air filled with grill smoke and lively chatter. Bright chaos! So different to Sweden. He felt a twinge in his chest, a pang of longing. If he'd been at home in Stockholm, in his apartment, he'd have been feeling peaceful and centred instead of wildly off balance. Here, everything seemed to be slanting the wrong way, or maybe it just felt like that because Emilie wasn't by his side.

He moved through the bar, looking for her pale pink dress. He'd seen her on the beach with Melinda, watching the dancing, but now…? Nowhere to be seen. His jaw was aching. Had he been grinding his teeth? He pushed through the tables to the steps, looking left and right. If he had to trawl every inch of the beach, he was going to find her. He had something to say, something she needed to hear…and maybe when she heard it, it would make whatever was wrong between them come right again.

* * *

Joel stood at the water's edge, staring. Beyond the edge of the bay, lights were starting to wink and shimmer, bars and restaurants and houses settling themselves for the night. Why was he alone? Had he done something wrong, something to upset her? He couldn't think of what it could be, but his belly was churning and churning. *Where* was she?

He turned, looking back towards the bar. The interior was golden, strings of bare bulbs glowing, candle lamps flickering on the tables under the wide canopied deck. The chatter was a low burble, eclipsed by the mellow reggae number that was beating a path across the sand. For the umpteenth time, he scanned the guests for a trace of pale pink dress. Nothing! There was a knot of people beyond one of the braziers. Maybe she was with them, obscured by someone tall. He started walking, but as he drew level with the fire, he could see she wasn't there. Desolation flooded his veins. He turned away, staring into the glowing globe, feeling its warmth, losing himself in the intricate-cut design and in the dancing flames behind. Where *was* she?

'Joel…'

Emilie! He looked up, heart lurching, stumbling, fizzing. She was walking towards him, hair streaming behind her, dress flowing, a dark wrap sliding off her shoulders. He moved towards her, legs shaking, trying not to look ridiculously overjoyed. 'Hello, stranger! I've been looking for you.'

Her face seemed milky pale in spite of the flickering orange light from the fireball. 'I'm so sorry. I was on my way to find you, but the bar manager caught me. He asked me to clear my stuff out of the storeroom.' She shook her head a little. 'I felt so bad! I'd completely forgotten about it!'

He hadn't thought to check the storeroom! Maybe she hadn't been avoiding him after all. He felt a smile straining his cheeks. 'You should have come for me. I'd have helped.'

She nodded. 'I know.'

It was so good to see her, but she wasn't smiling. He tuned in to the familiar reggae track pulsing through the air. Maybe he could make her smile. He slid his hands to her waist, moving his body to the music. 'Do you wanna dance with me, baby?'

'Are you drunk?'

'No!' There was the faintest glimmer of mischief in her eyes. 'Why?'

A smile touched her lips. 'You told me you only dance when you're very drunk.'

He laughed. Was it really only a week ago

that he'd caught her dancing in the kitchen? At least she was smiling now. 'Well, there are exceptions, like when I've been missing someone like crazy and can't wait to hold her in my arms.'

Something stirred behind her eyes and then her hands landed lightly on his shoulders. 'I'm sorry for abandoning you. It was wrong of me.'

She smelt so lovely. He wanted to pull her into his arms and kiss her, but first, he wanted her to dance, wanted to dance with her. He pushed her hips to the left and then to the right, encouraging her to sway with him. 'You had people to see, a baby to make a fuss of. I didn't mind.' Could she see the lie cowering behind his eyes? 'The main thing is you're here now and I'm glad because there's something I need to say…'

She seemed to catch her breath, and then her eyes fastened on his. 'I've got something to say too.'

'Oh…?' Whatever it was, it was making her nervous. He felt his heart slipping slowly downwards. 'Well, maybe you should go first?'

Her hands fell from his shoulders, then she stepped back a little, pulling at the edges of her wrap. Her smile, when it came, was small and tight. 'I've found a café…well…a potential anyway. It's in the neighbouring village to my grandmother's.'

'Right…' His stomach clenched. If she was thinking about the café, then… 'That's great!'

'It could be…' She was biting her lip. 'And Tom's come through with the money. I got an email this morning.'

His heart slipped lower, beating hard, panicky beats. *Tom!* It was good that Tom had come through, but it was not what *he'd* wanted. He'd wanted to be the one to help, the one to… He swallowed hard, trying to sound pleased. 'So, you're on your way to a new adventure.'

She blinked. 'Well, nothing's sealed yet, but at least I know what I'm going to be doing when I get back.' Her eyes held his for a long moment. 'So I need to focus on that now, put in some groundwork.' Her tongue hovered over her lower lip. 'Joel, what I'm trying to say is that I don't want you to be offended if I'm…if I'm too busy with things from now on to…to continue with…us.'

His legs turned to rubber. His breath seemed to be stuck. He felt his heart curling into a tight ball. Was she drawing a line under things? That couldn't be right. It *couldn't* be!

Her fingers were winding into her wrap. 'We've had fun though, haven't we, this past week, hanging out…?' Her gaze fell from his and then she was looking up at him again, a smile struggling on to her lips. 'You've been so lovely and so kind… And you've helped me to forget about Tom and…' she swallowed '… being with you has felt like…a little holiday.'

He clenched his back teeth hard, forcing back the tide of pain that was rising and rising inside him. She thought they'd been hanging out… *Hanging out?* Right enough they'd said 'no strings', but it had never *felt* casual. No kiss, no touch had ever felt less than… and what about the light he'd seen in her eyes so many times? What about the way she'd touched him when they'd been making love? And it *had* been making love…for him. Even though he'd been confused about Astrid, it had always felt *real* with Emilie and he'd thought that it was the same for her too…

Kristus! How could he have got it so wrong? What was he supposed to do now? His heart was in his throat. His temples were pounding. All this time he'd been waiting for his walls to come down, but he'd never thought it would be *these* walls, the walls he'd somehow built with Emilie.

'And…' she was still talking '…hopefully, you'll find some closure over Astrid soon.'

His jaw went slack. There was no point telling her he'd resolved those feelings…not now.

He quashed a sudden bizarre impulse to laugh. He drew a breath, battling to keep his voice steady. 'Yes. Hopefully.' The noises around him were coming at him in throbbing waves. The sand seemed to be parting under his feet. If only he'd had more experience with women, with love, so that he knew what to do now... but he was clueless, floundering. A piece of timber shifted inside the fireball, sending a plume of bright sparks flying up into the air. He looked up, watching them. If only he could have been flying with them, disappearing into the dark sky. Escaping...

'So, you had something to say too?'

He met her gaze. Her eyes looked large, lustrous...beautiful. He wouldn't be able to look into those eyes every day for the next week. It would hurt too much to see her every day and not be able to hold her or kiss her. He'd have to go... He'd leave in the morning, first thing. He pressed a hand to the back of his neck. 'I wanted to say that I'm leaving tomorrow.'

'Tomorrow?' Her face blanched. 'I mean, that's sudden!' She swallowed. 'Has something bad happened?'

'No...nothing bad.' He dropped his hand and tucked it into the pocket of his chinos. 'It's just that a series of business meetings I'd fixed up in Miami has been pulled forward...'

Only the *pulled forward* part was a lie. The Miami meetings were genuine. He'd tacked them on to the end of his trip since he'd been flying back to Stockholm via Miami anyway. Leaving Buck Island early meant he'd have to kill time there, but he could hire a boat, cruise around the Florida Keys for a few days. Maybe it wouldn't be so bad. 'It's why I was looking for you…to tell you…but it seems like it's all working out for the best.' He sawed his teeth over his bottom lip. 'With me gone, you won't have to cook at all, so you'll be able to focus on your plans, which is good, right?'

She looked stung and that stung him right back. What was happening to him? He'd just lied to her about why he'd been looking for her and now he was sounding bitter. He hadn't meant to sound that way, but he was hurting as he'd never hurt before and it was hard keeping his voice steady, never mind controlling what came out of his mouth.

He looked over to the bar, lively with happy, chattering guests. The party would be finishing soon and then they'd be able to head back to Buck Island. He'd walk Emilie back to the cottage and say goodbye, and that would be that. Until then, he would have to endure his pain, hide it somehow, because Emilie didn't deserve his sharp, raw edges. They'd been having a fling and now she'd drawn a line under it. It wasn't her fault that he'd fallen in love, wasn't her fault that he was falling apart. He drew a steadying breath, forcing out a smile. 'Hey! We should go get a shot of rum to toast the quiet café. You can tell me more about the place you've seen.'

She seemed to hesitate and then gave her wrap a little tug. 'Sure, why not.'

CHAPTER TWELVE

WHAT HAVE I DONE?

Emilie sat up gasping, shoving at the quilt,
scrambling out of bed, then scrabbling under
it for the sandals she'd kicked off the night
before. *Joel!* She *had* to see him. Letting him
go without saying something…anything other
than the nothing she'd managed last night was
wrong, just…*wrong*!

She touched a strap with her fingertip and
stretched more. A spreading panic was making
her fingers clumsy. Flashbacks were swarm-
ing into her head… Joel swaying to the music,
hazy-eyed…the warm pressure of his hands
moving her from side to side…that excruciating exchange…leaving…business meetings
in Miami…rum shots in the bar…telling Joel
about the café in Salton…the dull thud of her
words…the momentary brightness in his smile
as he'd touched his glass to hers…

'You'll be a great success, Emilie…'

Her fingers closed around straps and she pulled, shuffling backwards. She couldn't stop the memories unspooling…the cool breeze and the roar of the power boat…the dark water shifting and the inky sky. His silence and scuffing shoes…the path and the lights… Her mute tongue…her breaking heart. Breaking and breaking, silently. His eyes…dark and shuttered…at the door…that moment…that heavy, heavy moment… His lips grazing her cheek…the Swedish words he'd murmured… his shoulders stiffly moving…his pale khaki shirt…retreating…

She'd watched him go, too choked to breathe, telling herself that it was for the best. But if it was for the best, why did everything feel wrong? For once, she'd listened to her head, decided that stepping back was the only way to protect her heart, but now her head was spinning, waltzing her heart around, faster and faster, and she wasn't sure of anything any more. Except that it wasn't right to have let things end like that. A sob struggled up her throat. After everything they'd shared, it just wasn't right.

She pushed her feet into her sandals, hopping over the floor to hook the strap around her heel, then she grabbed her cardigan and flew out the door, stabbing her arms into the sleeves as she ran along the path through the trees. It was early, surely early enough to still catch him. It *had* to be, because… One minute he'd been asking her to dance, that warm, fond look in his eyes, and the next minute, he'd told her he was leaving the next day.

In between those two things, she'd delivered her little speech about the café and about how she couldn't see herself having time for him in the coming week and, while she'd been speaking, the sweet light had seemed to drain from his eyes. He'd been shocked, of course, but there'd been something else too, something he'd been trying to hide. She'd seen it, noticed it, but it had been so hard getting her own words out—heartbreaking words—that she'd had to push past it, blinkering herself. But now all she could see was his torn face and all she could feel was panic jabbing in her veins. Had she got everything wrong…made a terrible mistake?

She broke through the trees, running hard through the soft glow of morning, racing up the wide path towards the house, legs burning, heart pounding. She paused for breath, then took the pale steps two at a time, stumbling through the open door. Everything was silent. She ran to the kitchen, skidding to a halt in the doorway. It was pristine. Was he still sleeping?

Please, let him be sleeping.

She spun on her heel, racing through the hall, up the stairs and… The door of his room was ajar. She touched her chest, inching forward until the handle was right there. She closed her eyes, listening, heart pounding, then she pushed the door open and her heart stopped altogether.

The bed hadn't been slept in.

Joel! She stared at the undented quilt and the smooth pillows, tears burning in her throat. She stepped closer, staring, blinking… They'd made love in that bed, showered together in the luxurious wet room, but now the emptiness was overwhelming. *No!* Not emptiness. It was something deeper, darker and more desolate. Was it in the room, or was it inside herself? She turned, wiping her eyes, scanning the room, looking for…what? The wardrobe doors were hanging open, flung wide. The hangers were jutting every which way as if he'd ripped the clothes right off them.

He ripped his clothes off the hangers…

Her throat closed. She sank on to the ottoman, felt a sob shaking in her belly. If he'd been packing for a business meeting, he would have been more measured. He would have closed the wardrobe doors. She bit her lips together, felt tears sliding down her cheeks.

There weren't any meetings in Miami. He'd made it up. *Why?* He'd got back to his room last night, thrown his things into his case and left because... Because of her? Because she'd told him it was over? She stared at the hangers, felt her lungs collapsing. *Oh, God!* Good with evidence, but so, so poor with intuition! She'd hurt him...made it impossible for him to stay... which meant he cared, had feelings for her... the kind of feelings she hadn't allowed herself to believe in. Why hadn't he said anything?

Oh, no! She dropped her head into her hands. *That* was what he'd been going to say on the beach! *That* made sense, way more sense than his sudden announcement about leaving. It tallied with the warm delight she'd seen on his face when he saw her walking towards him. It tallied with the gentle way he'd tried to get her to dance with him and with what he'd said about missing her like crazy. It tallied with everything—with everything she knew about him and with everything she'd felt when she'd been with him—with the way he'd made love to her, with the way he'd looked after her when they'd been sailing and snorkelling, even with the careful way he'd carried the cake box.

Melinda had tried to tell her. *'It's plain to see. You only have to look in his eyes...'*

But she'd closed her eyes, because she'd thought she was falling into her old ways, weaving fantasies out of thin threads, instead of being strong and independent. She'd convinced herself that what she'd seen in Joel's gaze couldn't possibly have been real. She'd told herself that taking himself off without her, that never spending the night, had been his way of reminding her that what they'd been sharing *was* a fling and nothing more. Why had it been easier for her to believe that he couldn't have real feelings for her than to believe that he could?

Melinda's words fell into her ears, drumming like rain. *'You need to believe that you're enough...by yourself... You don't always need a passport.'*

She got to her feet, swaying for a moment, then pacing. She'd made baby Ben's cake because she'd wanted to show Melinda and Erris how much she appreciated their friendship, but could she deny that there hadn't been something of the passport about it too? Always that feeling inside that she had to earn love, that she wasn't worthy of it in her own right. A sad ache filled her chest. It was the way she'd always felt. From that indefinable moment in childhood when she'd become self-aware, she'd felt aware of her isolation. She'd always felt like an atoll in the sea of her own family.

She broke step, drawing in a slow breath. Maybe her sisters had never meant to exclude her and perhaps her parents had tried to make a fist of things when they'd discovered they were having a late baby, but the fact remained, she'd felt what she'd felt and she'd been carrying those hurts around for ever. They'd shaped her. She'd spent her life trying to be noticed, working hard to make sure it happened, but always feeling so insecure about it, as if the ledge could crumble at any minute. Clinging to that ledge, and to people, needing validation all the time...

She gathered her hair, twisting it round and round, swallowing hard. It was a choice though, wasn't it, dragging those chains around? She didn't have to do it any more. They were too heavy, and they'd cost her too much. She was twenty-nine years old, desperate to have a family of her own, but she had to grow up, *be* a grown-up. She had to start believing that she was enough...*really* believe it.

She went to the wardrobe, ran her fingers over the hangers. On the beach with Joel the day they'd played the trust game, she'd told him that she trusted people too easily, but that she was going to change and he'd said, *'Don't...'*

She closed her eyes, felt tears welling behind her lids again. *Don't change...* That was what he'd been going to say. She could see it now, so clearly. He'd come straight out with it, tried to cover it up with the woolly wall bee hoax, but it had sprung from his mouth so spontaneously that it had to have come from the heart. He hadn't known her then at all, not really, and yet somehow he must have known instinctively that he didn't want her to be anything other than what she was, which was...enough!

She rubbed at her eyes and her nose, staring into the wardrobe. The hangers were straight now, lined up, one inch apart. She hadn't noticed herself doing it. She closed the doors and turned, staring at the unmade bed. If Joel had left, he'd have taken the power boat because he had luggage.

She sniffed, wiping her cheeks with the backs of her hands. The thing was, she hadn't heard a boat leaving. Her heart thumped a single loud beat. She licked her lips. She'd been tossing and turning all night, barely sleeping, and the jetty wasn't far from her cottage. Her heart thumped twice. Surely, she'd have heard the boat... Her legs started moving and then she was hurrying through the door, clattering down the stairs. She'd have heard the boat starting up…definitely…she would have.

Definitely!

She shot through the door, jumping down the steps, running down the path. Down, down, legs spinning, cardigan billowing, then it was the steps to the jetty and the short path through the trees with grit flying, nearly stumbling, slewing to a halt with a sob in her mouth.

The powerboat was there, rocking gently against the mooring, but there was no sign of Joel. She dragged air into her lungs, swallowing hard, moving forward, step after step until she was alongside. She scanned the cabin, the cream leather seats, the chrome and the polished walnut wheel and…a huge leather hold-all on the deck, not quite zipped up, a leather tag dangling. It was etched with his initials. Tears filled her throat, started spilling down her cheeks. He was still on the island! *Still here!* There was still a chance! *A chance!*

She looked at the dash again, then slipped off her sandals and boarded the boat. For the hundredth time she wiped her eyes, then she pulled the keys out of the ignition, balling them into her fist. She sucked in a long shuddery breath, then jumped back on to the jetty and picked up her sandals. He wasn't going anywhere now. Now, it was just a matter of finding him.

* * *

Joel raked his fingers through the sand, watching the tumbling waves. The breeze was cool this morning, stiffer, but it felt nice. The smooth boulder behind him felt nice too. Cold. Cooling his blood, calming him down. To think he'd got as far as throwing his bag into the boat! *Dumskalle!* The thump of the bag on the deck had broken his fever, brought him to his senses. Leaving wasn't an option when everything he wanted was here and he was going to fight for it, couldn't *not* fight for it. But waking Emilie at four-thirty in the morning to tell her that he was in love with her had seemed a bit inconsiderate, so instead, he'd walked round and round the island, watching the sky growing lighter.

Emilie! He'd wanted to tell her what was in his heart the moment he'd got back from Salt Island, but she'd seemed so preoccupied with the cake that it hadn't felt like the right time for a romantic declaration. The beach at dusk, with the brazier glowing and reggae music playing had seemed perfect, but then she'd hit him with her whole cooling-off speech. *Kristus!* He'd never felt pain like it, tearing right through him. He'd felt blind with it, delirious. How he'd managed to smile, toasting the success of her café, he'd never know.

He couldn't remember driving the boat back or walking her to the cottage. It was all a blur except…for that moment at her door. It was where he'd kissed her for the first time and, standing there again, her eyes on his, he'd wanted to pull her into his arms and kiss her senseless, but she'd set new rules and he wasn't the kind of man to cross a boundary like that. So he'd kissed her cheek, told her he loved her—*jag älskar dig*—and left.

Why had he said it in Swedish, knowing she wouldn't understand? His belly quivered. Because for a split second he'd felt scared that his love wasn't real enough or deep enough. Emilie had invested all those years in Tom and had lost everything. Loving Emilie came with a weight of responsibility. A responsibility to keep loving her, to take that love on a journey, with stops, like marriage, and a family. She deserved nothing less. In that desperate moment at her door, he'd realised that if he was going to try to change her mind, he needed to be damn sure of his feelings and he'd known last night, aching and miserable, that he'd been in no place to judge. But now he was.

He rubbed his palms on his chinos and got to his feet, felt warmth flowing through his veins. From the moment Emilie had dived on to the sand to help him with the runaway sail he'd felt his heart stirring. That exact moment when she'd caught his eye was the moment he'd fallen in love. He knew it now, but he hadn't quite seen it at the time. What he'd seen, what had taken him over, was a puzzle.

He'd thought of it as the puzzle of Astrid, a quest to understand how his long-term relationship could have died with barely a whimper, but really, the puzzle had always been about himself. He'd needed to find out who he was, needed to know that he could trust himself, and his feelings about the past, about his family and about Emilie. He'd had to lift a few rocks, peel back a few corners, but from the moment he'd straightened it all out in his mind, from the moment he'd understood the reasons for everything, his love for Emilie had flown free. And it was still there, shining away, but did *she* love him back?

He bent to pick up a cowrie shell. Last night, she'd pushed him away, but he'd *felt* her love flowing so many times, seen it in her eyes, felt it in her kiss and in her touch, that he had to believe in it. She'd been hurt so badly. If she'd been trying to protect herself, then it was understandable. They'd jumped in with both feet, going with the flow, but Emilie wasn't any more casual about relationships than he was. Maybe all she needed to hear was that he was ready to start talking about strings. If she needed time, reassurance, he could wait because he *was* sure. If pain was the body's way of telling you that something was wrong, then the pain he'd felt at the thought of losing Emilie was enough to show him that his feelings were true.

He checked his watch and started walking. By the time he got to Emilie's cottage, it would be six-thirty. She'd probably be up, drinking coffee on the veranda. Hopefully, she'd listen, let him tell her that he was in love with her. Was it too soon to tell her that he wanted a future for them, full of happiness and babies?

He felt a smile coming. At the party, watching her cradling Ben in her arms with that fond look on her face, he'd felt his heart blooming like it had that first night in the kitchen when she'd got the text about Ben's arrival. Her eyes had been glistening with happiness and he'd felt such a strange shock of emotion that he'd thought he was suffering with exhaustion. But it hadn't been fatigue. He knew that now.

It had been an awakening, a sudden unexpected recognition that he wanted a family of his own, a bunch of noisy kids, well, hopefully not *too* noisy! But he would never *make* them enter speed-cubing competitions…or any other competitions unless they wanted to. He'd simply let them be whatever they wanted to be, supporting them, encouraging them, but never trying to mould them into being anything other than what they were, because that was what love meant, accepting people for what they were.

He sighed, felt sadness aching in his chest. If only his father had been able to accept *him* like that. If Lars had respected his quiet nature instead of trying to make him into something he wasn't, then they might have had a better relationship. Emilie, kind-hearted as always, had said that maybe Lars had been trying to bring him out of his shell. He fingered the cowrie, felt a guilty shiver running along his spine. He'd only ever shown his father a cool, smooth surface. He'd kept everything inside, trying to make himself amenable, because Lars was loud and intimidating, but what if he'd actually told Lars how much he hated the competitions? At least it would have given Lars the chance to understand. He drew an uncomfortable breath. At the distillery Emilie had thrown him a curved ball. She'd said that maybe Lars found *him* intimidating. He stopped, shifting the heaviness around in his chest. So many shards and splinters seemed to be rearranging themselves into new configurations. Could it be that the disappointment he'd been reading in his father's eyes for all these years had nothing to do with the family business at all? Could it be that Lars was simply disappointed that they had never really got to know one another?

He weighed the shell in his hand, then backstepped into a lunge, pitching it up and out across the water. Impossible to know what was in Lars's head unless…he asked. A momentary unease stirred in his belly, but it was only the ghost of old resentments. He drew in a long breath. He could try talking to Lars. It might come to nothing but whatever the outcome, he'd handle it because he wasn't that shy, intimidated boy any more.

He felt a warm glow chasing away the heaviness. Emilie would approve of him reaching out to his father. She was all heart. One of life's creators—a warm, beautiful soul—who needed to understand that she didn't always need to be creating something for people to love her. He'd help her to see that she was perfect just the way she was, if she'd let him…

'Joel!'

Emilie? He spun round, felt his heart exploding. She was running flat out along the water's edge towards him, hair streaming behind her, pale cardigan flapping, wet splashes darkly peppering her pink pyjama shorts. For a beat, he couldn't breathe. She was coming for *him*, sprinting…in her pyjamas! It had to mean she loved him. It *had* to.

Hjärtat! Sweetheart!

For an infuriating moment his legs wouldn't work, then they started to move and he was running, heart racing and racing, legs going faster and faster, closing the distance between them until it was five metres, four, three, two, one, and she was launching herself into his arms, crying, kissing his face and his lips, over and over again and he was kissing her right back, breathing in her flowery, spun sugar smell, tasting the salt on her lips and the heat in her mouth, taking it all, taking everything until his head was spinning. He tangled his hands into the dark softness of her hair, pulling her closer, but it wasn't close enough, or warm enough, or deep enough. He cupped her face, kissing her eyelids and her cheeks, kissing away the tracks of her tears.

'*Jag älskar dig.* I love you, Emilie. I love you.' He kissed her again, his heart filling and filling. 'I love you.'

Her eyes were full of light and tears. 'I love you too. So much…' She was smiling and crying at the same time. 'I'm so sorry… I didn't mean to hurt you. I was scared…trying to save myself from…but I should have talked to you, not just…' Tears were streaming down her cheeks, breaking his heart. 'I can't believe I let you go…' She was biting her lips. 'Do you have to go?'

'No, no… Don't cry.' He smoothed away her tears with his thumbs. 'I'm not leaving.'

'So those meetings…?'

He felt a small pang of guilt. 'I do have meetings, but they're scheduled for after I leave here.' He took a breath. 'I just said I had to leave because—'

Her hands went to his face. 'Because I pushed you away and you were hurting…' Her lips touched his. 'No more hurting each other, okay? We need to talk…sort things out.'

Sorting things out was exactly what he wanted to do and now there was a whole week ahead of them in which to do it. He felt his heart lifting and lifting. Just being with Emilie filled him to the brim. And she loved him. She *loved* him.

He felt grateful, happy tears burning behind his eyes and he didn't care that she could see, because he was laying his heart on the line and it felt so good to be showing her all the love he was feeling inside. It felt freeing, like flying the hull… *No!* It was better than flying the hull, so much better. He smiled. 'Sorting things out sounds perfect to me.' He tilted her chin, kissing her softly. 'I have a few ideas about how we could make a start on that.'

She giggled, arching her eyebrows. 'They always say it's the quiet ones you have to watch.'

He laughed. 'You've seen nothing yet. Come on…' He caught her hand, meaning to walk, but her hand was a tight ball. 'Hey, what's this?'

She opened her palm. 'Keys to the boat.' Her lips were twitching. 'There was no way I was going to let you go without saying goodbye.'

A fresh burst of warmth filled his heart. He pulled her close, kissing her again. 'I'm definitely not saying goodbye.' He smiled. 'I seem to be tangled up in someone's strings and I kind of like it.'

Her eyes sparkled. 'I like it too.'

CHAPTER THIRTEEN

One year later...

'HEY, YOU...'

Emilie felt her heart jolt and skip. What was Joel doing, standing in the cottage doorway? He wasn't supposed to be seeing her until later. She glanced at the two marzipan figures she'd just finished making, supposedly a surprise, but it was too late now, he was walking towards her, giving her the full cute dimple treatment. It was impossible not to smile. 'Hey, but also...what are you doing here? I'm sure this isn't allowed... It's bad luck.'

'That's just silly superstition.' He was stepping behind her, sliding his arms around her waist, pulling her in. She snuggled against him, happiness surging through her veins. Being wrapped in Joel's arms never grew old. His lips were grazing her ear. 'I insist on saying good morning on our wedding day...'

Wedding day! She hugged the thought hard. A year ago, she'd thought her life was in ruins and now…she felt her veins tingling…now, she had a whole new future, a better one than she could ever have imagined. They might have started out as holiday lovers, they might have had to jump through a few hoops, but ever since she'd run into Joel's arms on the beach a year ago, it had been plain sailing.

The week they'd spent together before Joel had really had to go off to Miami had been filled with love and joy and laughter. They'd talked so much, opening up about everything. They'd sailed and swum. They'd explored more of the islands, but Buck Island had always felt like the best one. It was their special place because it was where they'd fallen in love.

It was why they were getting married on the beach, in the exact spot where Joel had landed his catamaran on the day they'd met. It was why she was making the surprise cake topper for their wedding cake. Two figures. A tall handsome one in orange swim shorts and life vest and a smaller dark-haired one in a swim-suit and sarong.

Joel was smiling into her neck. 'Am I see-ing what I think I'm seeing?'

'You are, but you weren't supposed to see anything until the wedding breakfast.' She wriggled herself round to face him, trying to look stern. 'It was *meant* to be a surprise.'

'It is a surprise!' He peered over her shoulder. 'They're fantastic, although...' his eyebrows drew in '...the Emilie figure isn't nearly sexy enough.'

'Flattery will get you everywhere.' She tipped her face up for a kiss, melting into the warmth of his lips, breathing in his clean, masculine scent. Joel had a way of making her feel special, of making her feel enough, perfect just the way she was. It was hard not to start believing in yourself when you were with someone who believed in you so absolutely, someone who took your dreams into their own heart.

Joel had encouraged her to buy the café in Salton. She'd set it up exactly the way she'd planned, but it hadn't been long before she was handing things over to a manager. Being apart from Joel most of the week had been too hard and, after he'd walked in one afternoon and dropped to his knee, proposing to her in front of all her customers, she hadn't had to think twice. He'd said he'd have asked sooner if he hadn't been worried that she'd think he was rushing things. *As if!* She slipped her hands to his face, breaking the kiss. 'So how are things up at the house? How's Grandma?'

He stepped back a little. 'She was in the pool with Lars when I left, talking his ear off.'

'That's Grandma! You think your father's larger than life? He's got nothing on Grandma!'

Joel laughed. 'It's entertaining to see a big man taken down by a little old lady.'

She slipped her arms around him, feeling a little swell of gladness. 'I'm so happy that all the family are here…' Her mum and dad had made it and her sisters with their husbands. Joel's family *were* full on, different to Joel, but they were good fun, and now that Joel had built some bridges with Lars, he seemed more centred, freer of spirit. Parents could so mess up their kids! She held in a smile. Hopefully, she and Joel wouldn't screw things up with their kids. Making a baby was their agreed honeymoon project.

'That's a very wide smile you're wearing, Mrs Larsson-to-Be.'

'I can't think why.' She stretched up, kissing him again. 'I'm only about to marry the most wonderful man in the world.'

He was beaming his dimple right at her. 'Of course. Right…yeah…you are.'

She laughed. 'I think you should go now. I've got to start transforming myself into a bride, and you need to go check on things at the house.'

'About that transformation…' His eyes were twinkling. 'I've got a little something for you…a surprise of my own.' He was reaching into his back pocket. 'It's why I came to see you.' A black velvet box came into view. He cracked it open, eyes on hers. 'I hope you like it…'

She looked down, felt tears prickling her eyes. It was beautiful. A fine gold chain with a single, substantial solitaire diamond in a simple setting. Understated, elegant. It was going to be perfect with her dress. She bit her lip. 'Oh, Joel. It's lovely. Thank you.' She met his gaze, felt her heart bursting with happiness, not because of the diamond, but because of him, because in a little over three hours he would be her husband. She slipped her arms around him, kissing him with all the love in her heart. It was going to be the longest three hours of her life.

'Are you nervous?' Nils was leaning in, nodding at the hipflask glinting in his hand. 'I've got some Dutch courage in here.'

Joel shook his head, smiling. 'I'm not nervous and I'd quite like not to be smelling of whisky when I kiss my bride, but thanks.' It had only been three hours since he'd last seen Emilie and he was missing her like crazy, aching to see her walking towards him. Loving Emilie meant missing Emilie. He'd learned that the hard way.

Encouraging her to go ahead with Café Hygge in Salton had felt right at the time. It was her dream and a damn good idea to boot, but even though he hadn't wanted to rush things or put her under any pressure, being without Emilie in Stockholm had been unbearable. So he'd bought a ring and taken the plunge. Proposing to her in Café Hygge surrounded by curious old ladies had been interesting, but worth it just to see that smile lighting up her face, the one that made her eyes sparkle, the one that stopped his heart every time. It was the smile that had stolen his breath on this very beach, in this very spot, a year ago.

He glanced at his bare feet, flexing his toes. Getting married on Buck Island had been the obvious choice. It was the first place they'd thought of when they'd started planning. They'd both loved the idea of a late afternoon wedding on the beach, followed by a relaxed wedding breakfast at the house. All they'd had to do was put out chairs for the small gathering. Erris had made the rustic driftwood arch he was standing under and Melinda and Kesney had woven flowers through it, whites and delicate pinks, rather different to the vibrant tropical displays they'd chosen for the terrace up at the house.

He looked up, catching his father's eye. Lars moved his head minutely. A nod. He nodded back. There was a smoothness between them now. Acceptance. It felt better. *Family!* He scanned the faces…his mother and his sisters… Stephen talking to Jemima and Rebecca, Grandma tipping him a leery wink. He held in a smile. She was a character!

He moved on. Erris and Melinda, beaming… Kesney and Will trying to hold on to a wriggly Ben. Emilie's parents were sitting shoulder to shoulder, holding hands. Emilie hadn't wanted her father to walk her up the aisle. She'd said that she wanted to walk alone… She'd said it was a sort of symbolic gesture, because it would be the last time that she'd ever walk alone… She was right! He had no intention of letting her go. Ever!

He straightened his shoulders, smoothing down his blue jacket. Johan met his eye and held up two thumbs. He smiled, feeling a glow in his chest. They were cool. He was glad that Johan and Astrid were happy together. Astrid had had to stay behind because Karl's health was up and down and she hadn't wanted to leave him, but they were cool too, friends, which is how they'd started.

'Look!' Nils was nudging his shoulder.

He lifted his eyes, heard his breath catch. Emilie was coming, walking through the sand barefoot, holding a wild bouquet of greens and pinks and whites. He couldn't move. His chest was too full to breathe. *Emilie!* Tears burned in his throat. She looked so incredibly beautiful. Her hair was pulled up softly, tiny white flowers woven in. Her ivory dress was simple, elegant, flowing, and around her neck, she was wearing the diamond he'd given her that morning. What would she say when she found out that his real wedding present to her was Buck Island itself? He held in a smile, heart swelling, watching her come closer and closer. He was saving that surprise for later. For now, all he wanted to do was stay in this moment, watching his future walking towards him over white sand, with sparkles in her eyes and that perfect smile, shining just for him.

* * * * *

If you enjoyed this story,
check out these other great reads from
Ella Hayes

Unlocking the Tycoon's Heart
Italian Summer with the Single Dad
Her Brooding Scottish Heir

All available now!